Dark Lantern of the Spirit

An Arthur Wilson & Benjamin Hathorne Novella

by
Max Beaven

To my parents for everything.
And to Savanna for believing in me.

Table of Contents

Part One

"As phantoms frighten beasts when shadows fall."

Dante Alighieri

Prologue

Miles

Deer Creek Range, Wyoming - September 1897

Dusk arrived, casting a deeper pall of gloom over the trees and undergrowth. Miles glanced upwards, the sky an uncertain mix of violet and gray. His position on the eastern ridge made even the lingering light seem to weaken. Following a well-remembered path of traps laid earlier that morning, he was nearing the last trap's location, the prior traps yielding nothing.

He sighed, wondering at the folly of listening to tales of a giant wolf wandering these very mountain ranges where wolves had not been seen for decades. An experienced trapper, Miles had hoped for a coyote pelt or two at the very least. Money was short and he had few skills to fall back on. Most folks found comfort as cities encroached, but they had little to offer him in the way of a trade.

Each trap lay as it had been set, the bait of rabbit entrails now likely in the stomach of some clever fox or other predator. The traps were over large for a fox but seeing each one empty and unsprung was becoming more disheartening as he neared the last. He had placed new bait carefully over each pan, intending one more venture out in the morning before moving on to try his luck in other areas. Wolf be damned.

The woods seemed unnaturally quiet and even small game appeared scarce. He reached into his bag, feeling for his flask as the dreary chill intensified. Occupied by his fumbling's, his foot slipped forward on the floor of needles that now covered shale rather than the forest floor. Unnoticed in the gloom, an outcropping of rock blocked the path forward. Miles regained his footing and with it he glanced around, wondering at how he deviated from a path he had now walked for weeks. The slope still loomed to his right, but he could not recall having to veer around any rock outcroppings on what had been a well-established game trail.

Miles glanced about, the gloom on this side of the ridge was making dark shapes of trees and undergrowth and somehow, he, a born outdoorsman, had gone off trail. Reaching for his lantern, he looked at the small reservoir of kerosene and sighed. Locating his final trap, and any potentially wounded animal in it was his first priority. Once there he could find the trail leading back to the logging road and then a short way to his camp.

Returning his attention to the outcropping, he placed his hands on the stone for balance and began rounding it to his left. After a careful shuffling of a few feet, his right hand abruptly lurched into open space, nearly taking his full

4

weight with it. Grasping and pulling with his left arm he regained his balance, a sharp intake of breath at the sudden fear of falling into what was now revealed as a deep cleft in the rock face. With that intake of breath an unrecognizable scent caused his body to react and now all his senses alert, his lizard-brain screaming, he carefully stepped back from the now menacing rock face.

Quickly unslinging his lantern, he lit it with shaking hands, feeling all the while a chill in his spine that had little to do with the dropping temperatures. The lantern lit and held aloft in his left hand, he faced the deep crevasse, rock surfaces casting moving shadows in the faint flickering light. His sole frivolity, the Dietz Beacon lamp was a gift from better days, now battered but kept with loving care nonetheless. Its small yellow light allowed Miles to look at the cave entrance, for surely that was what it was.

In the dim light, a blackened substance was revealed to coat the edges of rock entrance and preceding ground. Upon moving the lantern more closely, he quickly wiped his right hand on his trousers, recognizing old and dried blood more brown than black in the revealing light. Bits of fur and skin fragments hung where they looked to have sloughed off against the rough rock.

His right hand dropped to his side; the bone handle of his knife gripped with fearful strength. A strong breeze buffeted his back almost pushing him into the entrance, the trees lashing against each other, groaning trunks and the wild susurrations of the upper branches creating a cacophony in the erstwhile silence. His Sharps rifle banging painfully against his back where it hung from its sling. Looking wildly around, the whites of his eyes grown large, Miles tried to locate the source of his sudden apprehension then…nothing. The trees began to slowly sway to quiescence. The wind becalmed and the near silence restored.

A sudden presentiment, and Miles quickly turned again to face the rock face, his mind arrested in its attempt to understand and assemble the parts of the horror before him. Something gripped him with horrible strength, the abrupt shock of his body being furiously rent apart only becoming clear in that instant…

A last disconsonant thought, as from a short distance he believed he could hear the harsh clapping sound of his last trap snapping shut.

Chapter 1

Arthur

Casper, Wyoming - October 1897

I stepped out of Townsend Dry Goods into the fresh fall air of late afternoon. Light winds swirled the dust across the roads. Glancing south past the few mainly wood frame buildings that made up the town center, I saw a scattered few foothills before they disappeared into the fog and an obfuscated Casper Mountain. Hearing the tread of boots on plank, I turned back to see Olly coming down from the Grand Central Hotel, slightly less stable for drink. Oliver "Olly" Rice was the former County Sheriff.

Tipping my hat, I greeted him. "Afternoon Olly."

Taking a moment to straighten up and pull at his suspenders, he unsteadily inquired. "Have you been over to the Saloon to hear the news?"

"I have not, I imagine the drink is still sub-par?"

"It suits, it suits." He took a moment to focus on me. "Hank Miles has presumably run afoul of trouble, he never returned to his campsite, and some of the boys down at the saloon found his traps still up on the mountain."

Hank Miles, who for some unknown reason was known in Casper by his surname, was a frequent traveler through the town, often heading into the local mountains for a month or two to trap before heading to more promising climes. My few encounters with him were friendly enough, although he was usually taciturn and often without funds. "And your professional opinion?"

"I am no longer paid to give my opinion, professional or otherwise." Here he made a slight cough. "I'd say he met with a fall."

"Miles knows those mountains like no one else, I sincerely hope that was your otherwise opinion. As a professional I'd have my doubts."

"Well it is mine regardless, but this mystery is now your remit." And with a tap of his finger against the nickel star on my vest, he veered rather too widely past me and dropped off of the planks, just balancing himself to walk with all dignity down the middle of the road towards his home.

I wandered down towards the Grand Central, no particular destination in mind. It was one of those rare fall days, that made me think of home. Born in Marblehead, Massachusetts, this was about as far as one could get from cobblestone streets and ocean air. As my memories wandered, I came close to the saloon, raucous noise filling the air. I remembered the University in Boston. Walking down gaslit streets with my closest friend and seeing her for the first time.

I shook my head to clear it. The reason I was living in a frontier town so far from home was to put that all behind me. I nodded at a couple as they passed me on the raised wooden planking that served for a street on this corner of Center. I had been here in Wyoming since shortly before it was granted statehood. I made my way north and settled here in Casper. I couldn't say why. Perhaps I had simply traveled far enough, changed enough, or forgotten enough.

I had been a deputy sheriff here for some six years. My education at Boston University of Theology and the hard years after I left made an impression I suppose, and Natrona County handed me my nickel star. I walked into the saloon and glanced around. Everyone seemed pretty jovial, with luck there'd be no need for my services this night. I wandered by the faro tables. The usual mix of the disgruntled losers and the overly happy winners. I wondered who Olly had received his information from. All these years and I was still the 'New Englander'. Though I'd long ago lost most of my accent. It wasn't enough.

Given that all of these men were strangers in some sense to this part of the country, it always struck me as odd to be one of the outsiders. I approached the bar, requested a whiskey. Although on duty, no one would much care, and I'd nurse it at any rate. It was a better option than what passed for water in Casper.

The bartender, James, was a decent sort. We were mutual misanthropes. It served better in my career than his, but he hid it well.

"Here you are Arthur." Sliding the glass to me. I nodded in response.

There was a motley group of outcasts, gambling men and questionable women, as befit any frontier town. I'd seen my share on my travels before settling here. This was certainly not the worst I had seen. I had little cause to draw down on anyone and most, knowing my reputation would be hesitant to let things get that far. But you never knew who might come through town.

I sipped at the whiskey, just enough to put a flush on my cheeks. My real purpose was to see if I could catch any of the conversation that Olly had been privy to. Asking questions would most likely clear them off or urge them to silence. Most of the talk was the usual mix of tall tales, heartbreak and business. I decided to move myself to a small table towards the rear where a couple of the fellows were having a vigorous exchange.

As I sat, I could easily hear the exchange, at the point where the drink made them all speak expansively.

"No, he's dead, the wolf had 'em. I know Miles, he went up after it and got himself killed." I recognized Fergus, one of the regulars, and a given liar. It seemed this argument was still ongoing, or Olly had caught its beginnings.

"He probably wandered off; Miles never was set to stay in one place. Not since he lost Molly." This from Grant, an older gentleman and one who had business interests in the area. "He wasn't in the habit of telling anyone his plans or whereabouts."

"He sat right here and made me go over every sighting of that animal. I'm telling you he found it and now he's done." Fergus was now standing and with an index finger making his point by driving it into the table with each of his words.

There was a general commotion around the table as each voice was trying to be heard. As the group quieted down, I heard Leonard's voice. He was a common fixture in the Grand Central. Having come from money, he spent a great deal of time drinking and coming up with unwise business dealings with which to waste that wealth. "I talked with him a week back. I had an offer for him to join in on a mining prospect. He was flat broke but wanted to invest. He was definitely looking for some opportunity to bring in some money. Whether he decided on doing some panning or trapping, I couldn't say but I saw him heading into the mountains with his kit."

This last was enough to convince me that there was a reasonable chance that Miles might have met with some misfortune. I downed the rest of the whiskey. Although I have always remained apart from it, it is my town and I protect my own.

Chapter 2

Benjamin

Salem, Massachusetts - October 1897

I paused to admire the gothic architecture of the Green-lawn Cemetery Chapel, a recent development, but one that I welcomed for its elegance. It was the first of November. My visit to the family plot a monthly occurrence, and one I dreaded. My sister Abbie having died the previous year of consumption, but not before securing my word that I would visit the graves of our parents each month.

Abbie never realized what had killed our parents. Officially it was documented as a boating mishap. I had been with them when it happened, and for a month after I was kept insensate with morphine because my delirious rantings didn't fit with the public appearance the Hathorne's demanded of the family. Abbie spent a great deal of time at my side, and I often wondered if the grief and fatigue led to her succumbing to illness.

She never blamed me for what happened, or for surviving. I was even more devastated when she passed, and I blamed myself for it all. My precious Abbie. If she had seen what I had witnessed, she would never have had a moments peace. And for her, I reconciled with the "official" explanation, a storm and a family ill prepared for it. In reality, I devoted myself to the acquisition of knowledge that would one day allow me vengeance. For Mom and Dad. For Abbie.

I shook the memories and melancholy away and departed the cemetery.

My duty fulfilled for the present, I turned towards Orne Street and began the morning's walk towards Essex and the Peabody Academy of Science. The ocean breeze bringing a mixture of salt and chill, I admired the foliage at its Fall peak. Rich auburns, yellows, and varying shades of earthen colored leaves rolling down the lane. I'd watch as they'd sometimes gather in small whirlwinds of color before falling to a rest. It was, in fact, my favorite time of year.

I picked up my pace, my spirits lifted having left the cemetery behind. I greeted the few passersby and turned onto North Street, an occasional sail falling in and out of sight out in the harbor, as I passed over the North River. The clatter of wagons increased as the morning wore on. A new shipment of curiosities was meant to be delivered today, and I fully intended to be the first to glimpse its wonders.

As I approached the granite facade of East India Marine Hall, I felt the usual eagerness begin its pull. My family's wealth provided for the acquisition of materials for the collection and gave me unique access to its wonders. Most especially, the right of first refusal on those peculiar items that I needed for my particular school of interest. And I rarely refused.

I slowly walked down the aisles of glass enclosed specimens. I never tired of seeing things pulled from oceans I would likely never see. I could hear the hum of some discussion in the back, and it was clear that the day's delivery had arrived. I hurried to the back rooms, where boxes and unclassified items lay in various states of disarray.

"Good morning everyone." I said to the room at large. I passed by other society members and headed directly to the small desk I was provided. A small package lay atop it, addressed to Benjamin Hathorne, Esq.

It appeared my machinations had finally come to fruition. For some time, I had been trying to acquire a volume of some antiquity. It's owner, of European nobility, had refused to part with it. Luckily, I was informed of his rapidly deteriorating health. His descendants had little use for books, but were concerned about the declining family fortunes, and I was more than happy to assist.

After carefully removing the outer packaging, I removed the volume which had been wrapped in oil cloth. I peeled back a layer, and confirmed it was indeed the book I had searched for.

"Liber Ivonis," I whispered. The tome quickly disappeared into my leather valise. I left the building as quickly as I had arrived. I had work to do, and this was not the place to do it.

Chapter 3

Arthur

Casper, Wyoming - October 1897

I awoke to the creaking of wagon wheels and the yells of drovers. The county furnished me with a small cabin built at the bottom slope of one of the foothills leading up to the mountains. A trail passed close by to the north, where I was often greeted with the discord of travelers at the most inconvenient hours. Today, I peered out the window to see the morning sunlight gleaming off the winding Platte. There were comforts to be had.

The steam was coming off my freshly poured coffee, when the knock came. I considered playing possum, but even a small possum would fail to play in such small environs. The county provides.

"Arthur! Come on man, sun's been up for hours." Ah, Crawley Harris, my fellow deputy and inevitable disturber of poor possums.

"Come on in Crawley." I beckoned with my hand through the panes in the front door.

Crawley entered, shutting the door delicately but still

wincing as the cabin shook, dislodging a bit of sawdust. "I see the county has provided fine residences to us both."

I smiled and proffered a chair as I mimed pouring another cup of coffee. He nodded and glanced around the place. A single floor with a bed, a stove for heat and cooking, two cabinets and the small table we shared with our coffees.

"I think yours might be a sight finer than mine." He grimaced as he spoke. After a swallow of coffee, he sighed, "Sheriff Patton wants us up on the mountain. We've a missing trapper, and some hunters came across his traps...all sprung. Some with bits of animal bone caught in the jaws. Small though. Everyone knows Miles would never leave an animal in his traps and checked them like clockwork."

"What type of traps are we talking?"

"Long springs with about a 9-inch jaw spread." He used his hands to mimic the circular jaw size.

"What was he after? I've never seen him bring in anything larger than a coyote."

"Well that's where things get a little strange..." He paused to take another sip. "He was at the Grand Central and a few of the fellers got to gossiping about a supposed monster wolf that's been seen up on the mountain. Miles apparently bought into the talk and saw potential to erase some debt with what a rare wolf pelt would bring in."

"I overheard some of this talk. Was Inkton one of these fellers?"

'Inkton' was Shoshone and passed through Casper often to trade and more usually stop in at the saloons to tell tales. Inkton was short for Inkton'mi and as near as I could gather, was some sort of joke to the Shoshone.

"Oh, he was there from what I was told, but sitting quietly most of the night. This wolf talk has apparently been making the rounds for a few months on an off, Miles just happened to catch wind of it during one of his visits to the town." Crawley downed the rest of his coffee and stood, pushing his chair back and scattering a bit more wood dust about my abode.

"Well then, given the giant wolves a'prowling, I'll grab my shotgun and gun belt and join you outside momentarily."

Crawley gave a passing nod and headed out to see to the horses.

Chapter 4

Benjamin

Salem, Massachusetts - October 1897

I entered my study and closed the doors behind me. Once entered and having closed both the storm windows and curtain to ensure total privacy and silence, I removed the volume from my valise and its wax cloth wrapping. I set it down and began lighting the various lamps about the room. I then returned to the book and began to admire the craftsmanship. Books such as this were just as much works of art as compendiums of occult knowledge.

It was not bound in human skin but rather, the binding was beautifully and intricately done, and I spent minutes just admiring its bibliopegy. I was interrupted by a knock at the study door, before I even had the opportunity to open its cover.

"Yes?"

"Sir, I hate to interrupt but you have a delivery." Came the distinct chopped English of the family butler, Oliver. He had worked for my father and although I didn't approve, he had made an impassioned argument for continuing the arrangement. My father had left him quite an endowment, but he preferred to continue on in his duties. I couldn't bring myself to demur, especially given his loyalty and discretion.

I walked to the double doors and opening the leftmost door looked out to see him holding a large wooden crate. I gestured him in, not happy with a man of his age lifting a heavy item. "Oliver you should have simply called for me, not lugged it over here."

"Sir, it's not very heavy, just rather large. I believe it's a small item carefully packed." With this he set it down on one of the more worn carpets adorning the study.

"Thank you, Oliver, I can manage from here. May I ask who delivered it?"

"He announced himself as Tom Barton, from the Peabody, sir."

"Ah yes, good lad. I'll make sure he receives a tip when I return there." And with this I escorted him out. He was a good man, and although I felt sure he had a good idea of the nature of my studies, his calm British facade remained unperturbed. One would not know by looking at him whether he had any opinion whatsoever on any matter. Only the potential loss of his position had ever roused any passion in him.

I looked over the various stamps to try and decipher its origin. The Federated Malay States. Although I wasn't terribly familiar with that part of the world, I did have a

British contact there. I had met him in London during my travels abroad and we had come to an arrangement, but I had not received any correspondence from him for quite some time. I walked towards the desk and reached behind it to rifle through the bag of tools I kept there. Finding a pry-bar that would suit my purpose, I returned to the container and began working my way around the top with a careful application of leverage.

Removing the lid, I rummaged about the excelsior until my hands met a hard, semi-rectangular shape some ten inches in length. Pulling it from the shavings, my prize was revealed to be an intricately carved box made of an exotic wood with which I was unfamiliar. I placed this with care on the desk, and dived back in. I felt about until I found a thick envelope. This contained a letter from one Thomas Kincaid, my contact and a liaison to Malay for the British Empire.

The mysteries of the book had not even begun to be deciphered and here was another. I began to read.

Chapter 5
Thomas

Kuala Lumpur, Malay States - September 1897

Dear Benjamin,

I hope this correspondence finds you well. I shouldn't wonder if you were surprised to hear from me, given the time that has passed since our meeting in Hampstead. I believe the box contained within will more than satisfy our agreement. I suspect it is a unique find, particular to your field of study.

I should give you an account of its providence. It was acquired at great risk to myself, and I'm not at all certain all dangers have passed. I'm not a religious man, but if you find it to be of value, a prayer would not go amiss.

I was walking along the Gombak, a great muddy river that has a confluence with the Klang where the city resides. The humidity here is quite awful, but on this day, I had decided to wander about the various merchants and prospectors who gathered there. Goods you will see here that one could not find anywhere in London.

I encountered a small group who were having an animated conversation and walking closer, I picked up bits of pidgin English. A few Chinese were having it out with the locals. I interceded and was able to speak with one of the Chinese who had enough of a grasp of English to provide an explanation of the disagreement.

You should understand that a great deal of mining occurs here, and the Chinese in particular have a penchant for it. They had discovered a cave that had been worked in the ancient past. In the process of their exploration they had brought back a few artefacts they claim were littered about, in case they happened to be of some value.

The attempt to trade these items had excited the locals. Some of the Malays here have peculiar superstitions. They were angrily warning them off and telling them to return the objects. Out of curiosity I asked to see them. This further incensed the Malays. But they departed, my position possibly sparing me from an otherwise likely brawl.

It is here Benjamin, that I recalled at once our conversation. The items were of a strange almost jade-like stone, but darker and reacted strangely to the light playing over their surface. And the figures————such figures! The words you used to describe such things in the dim pub light were insufficient my friend. I don't have the words now.

The largest and most spectacular artefact I retained for you, the rest I have kept. They have such a pull on me!

There is an old man here known for his woodwork. When he saw the piece I intend for you, he reacted strongly but was almost gleeful when I commissioned him to create the box to contain it. I cannot say what meaning lay behind the carvings *he created, but I think you'll agree that they are uniquely beautiful. I will pack it carefully and ship it with this letter.*

Now, I come to the risks which I mentioned. I took this upon myself, and bear you no ill will, but I feel that I should warn you. Not long after I obtained the various statuettes and arranged them in my residence, I began to experience dreadful dreams. Such horrors I never imagined even in childhood when one still has the vivid nightmares of youth.

This is not the sole danger. When I dare to venture out at night I have been followed. Shadowy figures who move in a strange shambling gait. I believe the Malays who disputed the trade of these items have set about to punish me in some way. I have taken to carrying an Enfield revolver with me at all times. I will not let them have them back!

This has led to some fatigue on my part. I tire of this miserable ugly place. I have requested to return to London. Should that request be granted, I shall be back in Britain before this parcel reaches you. I hope it is of great value to your research! Should you find yourself in London again, look me up at my home. I will gladly show you the rest of the collection I have obtained thus far.

In the meanwhile, I plan to try and find the Chinese again. I will have them map out the location and then return to look for any other such figures. If my request is denied I may venture there myself.

Yours sincerely,
Thomas James Kincaid

Chapter 6
Benjamin

Salem, Massachusetts - October 1897

Having finished Thomas' letter, I felt a sudden trepidation. I had items and rituals of protection both here and in the reworked cellar. I knew, or believed I knew what existed beyond the sphere of human understanding. But, the arrival of the book and the box concurrently seemed more than happenstance.

I took the box and placing the book atop it, I headed to the cellar.

A wine cellar for my parents and their antecedents, I had given their collection away. Some to friends, some to relatives, and where they'd be of use——some as bribes. The door had been replaced, a sturdy oak door hung there, stained as to not stand out amidst the rest of the home's decor. It was locked and I kept the only key around my neck. As trustworthy as Oliver might be, I could not endanger him. He accepted this with the same insouciance as he would a request for tea.

I opened each of the two locks and carried the box and

book tenuously under one arm as I used the iron rail on the left side to balance me. Faint lamplight partially illuminated the stairs. Once I reached the bottom it was the matter of a few feet to reach a bench and set down my load.

I lit the lamp there and returned hurriedly to the door to lock it. The lamp caused the inside of the door to glimmer, as it reflected off the myriad of intricately designed sigils. It was the work of a month. I hand carved each channel and filled them with rare metals, blood, and other substances. It was one of many protections I had created here.

My study was my home, but the cellar was a shelter against eldritch horrors. Down here I felt like an alchemist of old. It was a workshop, a small library, and a fortress against the malefic————it served also to protect the people around me. Should I make an error, I would be the only casualty.

I brought the lamp back to the bench and lit another. Electric lighting was a relatively new occurrence, and I was looking forward to its slow encroachment. I admired Tesla and Edison and all their contemporaries, and would spend much time, and occasionally money at world expositions. I had been in Brussels earlier in the year and had funded some promising work. I often wondered, when the entire world was lit by electricity, would all the things in the dark disappear————or would they see it as a beacon.

Turning the box around I was able to admire its craftsmanship. Thomas was right, it was ingenious work. The series of channels intertwined with each other in such a way that the lamplight created small shadows around the features of the curious creatures designed there. They almost seemed to move. There was no lock, only a small iron latch. I lifted it and stifled a gasp as the relic within was illumined.

It was settled in velvet, and much as Thomas had described. Though words were not adequate. What being was the impetus for such a creation? Or was it purely the work of mad genius? It was some eight inches tall, and four wide. Thomas had said a dark jade, but I didn't think that was accurate. In my collection I had some pieces of volcanic glass, and I believed it was possible that this was similar. But the craftsmanship to work such materials, I doubted it possible there today, much less in the antediluvian past.

As I turned it over in my hands, the room darkened for a moment, and I glanced around. Wanting to assure myself that it was just a trick of the light, I recalled the almost obsessive tone of Thomas' letter. I carefully placed it in one of several lead lined coffers I kept for artifacts of unknown provenance. I made note to check in on him when time allowed.

I turned back to the book. It's origins in no doubt. Reaching to a shelf that contained several unused journals, I placed one beside the Liber Ivonis. Pen in hand, I opened to the first page of text and began to translate.

Chapter 7
Arthur

Deer Creek Range, Wyoming - October 1897

Our horses nickered as we crossed another switchback. I cantered over to the edge of the ridge, looking out over the still clear day to the small collection of buildings that made up Casper. Some 600 souls going about their business. A lifetime away from my more urbane upbringing. The chill at even this somewhat low altitude finding gaps in my wool overcoat.

"You're being pensive again." Opined Crawley.

"Where'd you learn a word like pensive?" I turned toward Crawley, where he was rubbing his nose against his jacket sleeve to hide his reddening cheeks.

"I pick up things, here and there." He looked up the mountainside. Due to our late start, we'd chosen a route that would traverse Casper Mountain to get to the range beyond, instead of following the road west and south. Either way, we'd soon cross a logging road, where the latest gossip had closely placed Miles.

Our trail soon neared the summit and began its winding

way down towards a valley set between the two mountains. I preferred to get this wild goose chase over with, but our meager lamps would be near useless once the sun set. So, it was likely that we'd camp in the valley.

Crawley spit over the side into the tree-line.

"I see your aim is getting better. Should our mammoth wolf appear, I shall cower behind your skirts until you phlegm it to death."

"Like I said…pensive." He moved his horse into a trot down the mountain side and I coerced my mount to follow. I briefly let my hand brush against the butt of one of the pair of Colt Frontier pistols that had been my constant companions since winning them years before in a game of Faro. Slung on the horse was a 10-gauge Winchester repeating shotgun, loaned to me by sheriff Patton for this venture.

Once the trail leveled off, we were in a small valley, clutched between the two mountains. The heavily forested slopes diffused the late afternoon light and made it feel like much later in the day. In addition to our mythological wolf, there were plenty of dangers about; Indians frequently gathered in large numbers in the forests to the south-east, outlaws often chose these forests to hide from the law, and other varieties of wildlife frequented the area.

"So, shall we set a camp here, or keep moving?" I was rather indifferent, but the light would soon become an issue.

"Well, had I not had to come to your cabin to roust you

we'd been at the road by now." Crawley seemed to still be nurturing a small grudge from my earlier comments.

"How far to the logging camp?"

"If we follow the slope west it'll gradually take us south and the camp will be some 5 miles from there..." Just at that moment a coyote began barking, joined by another, until the sound echoed in the valley making it hard to determine the direction they came from.

"Apparently we've disturbed the locals, I think we should take that as our sign to ride on." I tipped my hat in what seemed to be the general direction of the commotion, and with a sideways glance to Crawley. "Our apologies for the intrusion, we'll be moving on now."

Crawley rode silently on my left, as the sky darkened, we pushed our horses a little faster in accordance with the smoother terrain. I looked over to him, hoping he'd take my opening to speak. His eyes stayed forward, leaving it to myself to be the conversationalist.

"You're looking pensive again." Crawley's head snapped over to me, and I quickly grinned to disarm any barb.

"Well, I think that sometimes you feel you're smarter than most folks...and I don't like being treated as such."

Ahhh, again I've managed to misconstrue a social situation. "I apologize Crawley. I felt we had a rapport, and as such, a little good-natured ribbing wouldn't go awry."

He turned away again, sheepishness belying the big

man's imperturbable spirit. "All's forgiven, I just have a feeling about this trip…" He paused, looking about as if he'd momentarily lost his way. "Do you not feel anything out of sorts?"

In truth, since we'd entered the valley and the light had started to dim, I had started to feel uneasy. It had been a few hours now since we had heard the coyotes clamor, and without consciously noticing it, I now realized I hadn't heard any of the usually raucous sounds of the forest.

"We're getting close to the logging camp, it's probably just the proximity to men that has them off."

Crawley looked around again, his agitation starting to infect me, when I noticed a spot of light off to our south. "Look, lamplight, must be the camp." I pushed my horse forward, and I heard Crawley briefly pause before he joined me.

He smiled, "I guess I must seem foolish after all."

"Not at all, but once we get to the camp, I expect you to save your sputum…I'm still counting on you." This time he tipped his hat at me grinning. And then with a combined "yah!" we galloped towards the lights with our spirits rising as the small yellow glimmers swelled into view.

Interlude One

Deer Creek Range, Wyoming - October 1897

There was a shifting. Scree slid below the rockface to scatter in amongst the pine needles and other detritus of the forest floor. A crack resounded, and echoed across the mountain sides, and the crevice that resided in the rockface now had a new shape as rock continued to shift and fall. A more circular blackness now displaced the narrow cleft and if there had been one to see, they might have noticed the blackened and brown coating appearance of the falling and sliding rock, and tufts of hair and flesh that not even the carrion eaters of the forest would come near.

Chapter 8
Arthur

Deer Creek Range, Wyoming - October 1897

I awakened to the myriad sounds that accompany a logging camp getting ready for the day. A few men were noisily meandering outside the tent, that the foreman had graciously loaned Crawley and I, yoking a skidder to a pair of decidedly unhappy looking mules. I stretched and made my morning ablutions, before realizing I hadn't seen Crawley in our tent.

Waving at the lumberjacks as they sported an encumbrance of various tools up one of the trails that led up amongst the stumps of already felled trees, I wandered over to the foreman. He stood hunched over a variety of papers, strewn on a makeshift desk in front of his tent.

"Good morning Sir. Have you seen my fellow deputy this morning?"

He spat a brownish glob onto the ground, entirely too near his place of sleep for me. Pointing south and east, he replied "He asked for directions to that trapper fella's last campsite. I sent him that-away. Last place we seen him come from."

I glanced where he pointed and saw a line of unbroken trees clinging to a slope, probably deemed too steep for the loggers.

"Thank you, and again for the accommodation." He nodded and returned his attention once again to the preponderous pile of documents.

I looked toward where our horses were hitched and saw no sign of Crawleys' black roan. He must have found a passable trail. I saddled my mare and began a slow trot towards the tree-line to see if I could determine which way Crawley had passed. There…a gap in the trees, and what appeared to be a game trail. I headed to it, somewhat unsettled that he hadn't wakened me, worried that our banter had really created a gap between us large enough that he felt the need to venture on alone.

The beginnings of the trail, for it surely was a game trail, though not recently used, began within a small group of the few deciduous trees in the area. Colorful foliage standing out amidst the deeper green of the pines. A small carpet of fallen leaves lightly crunched under hoof as I slowly rode into the trees. Only a few yards in, and it was apparent that if I didn't want to subsist on a diet of needles and tree bark, I would need to dismount.

The pines overshadowed the path, and only occasional sunlight peppered the trail as the treetops slowly moved in the light winds. The quiet was only broken by the occasional shouts of the lumberjacks starting to fade in the distance and the slight creaking of trees. It was apparent that the trail followed an impression along the slope, making what would have been a somewhat steep incline perfectly manageable and probably enticing to Miles for use as a route in and out of the deeper forest.

Although widely traveled and proficient with firearms I was not a woodsman. Even in a frontier town like Casper, I sought the luxuries that were to be had. And those being few, I read more wilderness adventures than took part. It was nearing an hour, when coming across a muddy depression in the trail, I saw hoof prints. Even to a novice like myself they appeared newly imprinted and certain to belong to Crawley's horse.

"Crawley!" Hands cupped I shouted his name. The dense forest seeming to mute my shouts.

"Crawley!"

"Shush, you're louder than a rutting moose." Startled by a voice coming from the nearly impenetrable trees to my right, I tipped backwards in my saddle, as years of habit made my Colt appear in my right hand and I peered into the undergrowth. A pair of wizened hands pressed towards me out of the brush, followed by a wizened and grimacing face.

"Inkton! Damnation, you're lucky I didn't end you!" My heart beating, I holstered the Colt and wondered at what age it was appropriate for a heart to just give up and leave the rest of a person's body to deal with the stresses and startlement.

"You should not be here. I told your friend the same." He shook his head slowly as if in puzzlement at the stupidity of man.

Inkton's English was nearly as good as mine, and better than most men who settled in the frontier. I was given to understand that he had attended a missionary school while young, but aside from having a known fondness for drink and games, and suspicions of being an occasional mountebank, I knew little of Inkton from our encounters.

"You saw Crawley pass? Was he headed in this direction? Did he say where he was headed next?" While the words came pouring out in a torrent, a result of my sudden shock, in my head they were said with measured authority.

Inkton's hands made a soft pushing motion, telling me to calm myself. He looked saddened. Not at all the imp-like character I was used to seeing in the Saloon.

"He passed this way about two hours ago. I stopped him, the same as you. He did not startle like a frightened doe. But also, he did not heed my warning."

I sat up in my saddle, the branches clear in this stand, and looked about for a moment as if Crawley might materialize then and there. But there was only the sound of the trees and Inkton's silent appraisal.

"Will you heed me? I believe your man and the one he seeks are gone."

I looked forward again, hoping for some sign of Crawley, a churning sensation in my guts.

With a sigh I dismounted, and Inkton began his tale.

Chapter 9
Inkton

Dakota Territory - November 1856

"I have wandered a great deal since my youth. I have seen much and listened much and back then I spoke little. After I left the school of the missionaries, I could not find my way. I was separate from my people. I listened and learned languages, and for a short time found a living translating between the tribes and your government.

As the open lands shrunk, and our people with them, I was no longer of much use. But still I would listen. I hoped to find a path for myself and a greater wisdom.

I ventured across the Dakota Territory, it was not then as it is now. There was still much that was wild. I was able to trade and interact with a great many peoples. Learn some of their tongue and their stories.

I learned of Issa and Coyote, of the Nimerigar of my people, the yee naaldooshii of the Navajo and many of the things I had forgotten to fear as a child. There are many tales, and many are the same across the tribes, the names simply change.

Now indulge this old man, I cannot help Crawley as he was driven on by a courage not tempered with age and wisdom. But you, I think, can still be deterred from this path.

I came to these mountains. Alone, and still looking for answers. In a late afternoon, I came across a small war party of Northern Cheyenne. Their blood was up, but after a few words, they saw I was no threat and we spoke of their purpose.

They had hunted these mountains, and the game was plenty and their interactions with your people congenial, considering the little time passed since the battles at Platte Bridge Station. Most of the larger tribes scattered, their chief believe they could survive free in these hills until game fled the coming winter.

But towards the end of summer, game suddenly became scarce. Illness spread through the camp, and with desperation many youths joined hunting parties passing through the forests and mountain sides to find food for the people.

Summer had become Fall, and now a single brave returned. His mind was broken. He insisted that the others of the party had found the entrance to ⬚htóno'omēē'e and something pulled them in. His ramblings were dismissed, and it was felt that his party had been ambushed, and he had been unmanned. So it was that a larger party was going into these same mountains to give battle to their enemies.

I asked to join them. I do not know what ill-advised temperament prompted me, but here was possibly another story and they were willing to accept me. A simple bow and knife I carried on me, next to their war shields, spears and rifles. Looking back, I was a fool.

We climbed higher up into the dense trees and followed game trails, looking for one said to be on the stone of the slope itself. As we rode, the darkness between the trees seemed unnaturally devoid of light, and the wind's fury rose. A call from our right, led us to a brave astride a path on the mountain side. His face was nearly to the ground, trying to decipher tracks in the gloom.

He pointed, north, and again we moved, the slight sounds of weapons being drawn and readied swallowed by the winds. We moved quietly, though any human would not have heard a word spoken above the noise of the trees lashing each other. We followed our scout, as he in turn followed the trail. The stone seemed to have shaped itself into a shelf for nature to have an expedient path. Then, as now, I felt it an ill omen.

The slope was thick with trees to either side, the geological wonder that carved our path from the very mountain, left us with a steep, likely unclimbable slope to our right, and a much gentler slope to our left. From there the miles of forest traveled westward until becoming ever more sparse in the foothills below.

The scout raised a hand, and we all gripped our weapons, our uneasiness having grown as the miles had passed. The evident leader of the group moved forward. I could barely make out the back and forth between the two, but a decision being made. The leader waved us on, creeping forward, perhaps less a need for stealth, than fearful anticipation.

And here is where my story may seem to you the lunacy of an old man, and perhaps that night did rob me of some of my sanity, but I swear to you…at peril of your life what I say is true.

Darkness had fully enveloped the mountain, and torches were lit, though they struggled against winds that should have been tamed by tree and stone. I could now make out the silhouette of a rock outcropping. It was perhaps 20 feet high and it incongruously thrust out of the side of mountain, ancient granite with striations that gave it the appearance of a forceful birth.

As our leader moved his torch closer to it, I could now see a darker niche in the center that absorbed all light and made it hard to distinguish its shape from the shadows cast on the stone surrounding it. The Cheyenne pulled a large jawbone club from within his buffalo cloak, its aged brown edge spotted with chips and darker stains, testifying to its provenance. He waved, and two more Cheyenne brought their torches closer, their off hands gripping spears with white knuckles.

The next moments were jumbled, uncertain images of dark mottled gray emerging from the darkness of the rock, lashing, rending, and tearing…a cacophonous confusion of death and blood. The leader was gone in an instant, pulled into the rock, his torch falling from his hand creating a kaleidoscope of images, as the other Cheyenne were quickly grasped and pulled apart as though by some giant unhappy with his toys. In those few instants, I thought I heard two gunshots, and saw what looked like weapons thrown into the entrance of what I now too believe to be hell.

I was rooted to the spot, having been at the outer circle of warriors, on the downward slope facing the rock, unable to grasp what was happening. The other Cheyenne flew like untethered marionettes towards the dark opening in the rock and only a sharp tug on my arm from the youngest of the warriors drew me away. We scrambled down the slope, falling without care and rising again to continue to run until at last, the trees thinned, and we slowed.

We turned as one, looking back into the dark forest, the wind here on the outskirts almost gentle. Panting hard I looked at the brave, seeing his widened eyes and the tears that fell for his brothers. I put my hand on his shoulder, grasping tightly. The only thanks I could give at that moment.

And this is nearly the end of my tale, I have not told it before, and it is for your life that I tell it now. The Cheyenne warned me not to accompany him as he returned to his greatly diminished tribe. He believed that with no one else to blame, a Shoshone who had borne witness to the slaughter would also bear the brunt of their rage and sorrow. From other travelers, I heard his tribe moved southward that very night. My people, with all their different names, and different words, now feared the mountain and kept well away. It has been so ever since. After saying farewell to perhaps the only person on this earth to face such a thing and survive it, I headed north alone."

Interlude Two

Deer Creek Range, Wyoming - October 1897

The thing in the darkness dreamed. And hungered. It had found…sentiences that could sustain and grow that part of its form that existed in the outside. Reaching out from its dreams, it sensed others nearby, perhaps soon it would feed again.

It recalled when it, and others of its kind, were brought these things and more and the need to exert its form to consume sustenance was rare. Then pain and light and conflict that shattered the world. It found itself here, where it had slept and dreamed, and dreamed and slept, until a part of it awakened to hunger.

The mass in the darkness seethed and churned and with a sudden furious motion…shed a part of itself. Now, in the small concavity that sat just a short distance from faint light that entered through the enlarged crevasse, a second writhing mass began agitated movements.

Reliance on the lesser things that approached it from time to time throughout the millennia, was coming to an end. The thing in the darkness recalled a form…and this new mass began to shape itself.

Taking tentative steps, like a toddler learning to walk, from the cave entrance, a man emerged.

Chapter 10
Arthur

Deer Creek Range, Wyoming - October 1897

I took small sips from my canteen. Inkton had taken to rubbing on his pouch and quietly muttering. His queer behavior was beginning to put my nerves on edge.

It was nearing noon, and the sun's rays were just beginning to peak over the summit. It did little to warm the chill that seemed to seep from the forest floor.

"How much farther?" I switched the shotgun to my right hand, to relieve the tension I was developing from the tight grip.

He stopped and looked around. I was unsure of what landmarks he was using as a guide as it all appeared to be endless pines and the unbroken trail, when he replied. "About another half hour at this pace."

Switching the shotgun back to my dominant hand, I thanked sheriff Patton silently as the oiled lever action smoothly chambered a shell. Inkton glanced over and nodded, possibly in approval. He'd loaded a single paper cartridge into his carbine some time ago. He suddenly grew alert, drawing the butt of his carbine to his shoulder.

"Something is coming."

Although I had my doubts about the near mythical wilderness senses of the Indians, I also had a strong instinct for self-preservation. I pulled the butt of my shotgun in tight and moved up against the higher slope. The stone that made up the path was 3 to 4 feet wide in spots and Inkton was able to brace himself against a barren pine tree to my right, giving us a clear firing lane and room to maneuver.

The path curved slightly some 100 yards in front of us and it felt like some minutes passed before I saw a figure lurching toward us, walking unsteadily as though drunk. The sunlight was directly overhead, but still the thick trees created a gloom on the pathway. As the figure neared us, I began to make out the rough features of a man.

"Crawley!"

"Stay! Keep your gun trained!" Inkton hissed.

I looked from Inkton to the figure of Crawley and back again, doubts causing me to hesitate to go to my friend's aid. For clearly, he was unstable from his experiences, and needed help.

My indecision was broken by the loud report as Inkton fired his carbine, he had already inserted another cartridge and was capping the nipple getting ready to fire again when I looked back towards Crawley.

He stood in the path, now stock straight, and I could see an indentation where the ball had entered his left pectoral. But as I watched no blood poured from the wound and Crawley's eyes now intently focused on us. His eyes... something was very wrong with his eyes.

"Fire!" Yelled Inkton as his Sharps discharged again, and he began the now seemingly interminable process of reloading.

I saw Crawley start to walk towards us again, his steps still faltering, but apparently unhurt and unaware of the second hole in his right cheek from Inkton's last shot. I fired towards his center mass, the shot leaving a grouping of pockmarks in his shirt from this distance, as I quickly levered another shell into the chamber.

He unsteadily closed in, and briefly standing in a rare ray of sunlight I could see...finally see, his eyes. They were a dark mottled gray, that seemed to ripple with movement an uneven surface like the fissures of a brain I had seen in University. I fired again in shock, this time the shot pattern much closer and Crawley, or this thing that had been Crawley, didn't appear fazed, but did stagger from the shot.

He seemed to be moving by using some other sense, because Inkton's third shot eradicated that horrible left eye. An odd depression formed where the ball hit, not at all like the gunshot wounds of my experience. A translucent fluid leaked from it as the Crawley thing moved the last step towards Inkton, whose tremulous hands were trying to load a fourth paper cartridge. He was still some ten feet from us, and it was then, my doubts of Inkton's tale, my logical reasoning, were lost.

Crawley's right hand lashed out with such speed that my eyes couldn't follow it. Against all sane laws, his arm pierced Inkton through his throat, lifting him against the pine at his back. An appendage of unreal elasticity, the same motile grayish color of those appalling eyes, now extended to unnatural length from the thing's arm, protruding through Inkton, pulping the cartilage of his throat. Only his exterior neck muscles holding the weight of his body, with savage will Inkton rolled his eyes towards me.

I let out a small mewling sound that I had never heard from myself before, and then, God help me, I ran.

Chapter 11
Benjamin

Salem, Massachusetts - November 1897

The last few weeks had passed quickly. During the day I attended to my duties at the Peabody, and by night I translated and worked materials as required. Additional relics and volumes had arrived piecemeal. Each adding to the breadth of my understanding. I had made great strides towards acquiring the knowledge that I hoped would one day allow me to avenge my family.

Growing increasingly concerned, I had also sent word to Thomas. I received no reply. I attempted to follow up with the British authorities in Kuala Lumpur but was discouraged to discover that he had disappeared. They believed he had either abandoned his position, or that some villainy had been done by the locals. I had not the time to travel there myself, but instead reached out to some of my other acquaintances in the area. I had little hope for him.

This morning was full of gloom. A chill breeze blew in from the ocean, promising rain or possibly snow. It scattered the fallen leaves and whistled through bare branches.

It was the beginning of another day at the Peabody, and I was ready to focus all my attention on the work there.

As I neared the granite face of the hall, I saw one of the clerks waving for my attention, a telegraph in his hand.

"Telegraph." Benjamin sighed. Here we were, miles away from the birthplace of the remarkable new telephone, and yet, expense prevented us from having the use of such a device. I maneuvered around the various workers and their freight, to reach young Tom Barton.

"Telegraph for you Mr. Hathorne." His voice chipper with the yet undimmed enthusiasm of youth. He handed over the telegram, now slightly more the worse for wear from his gyrations with it.

I began to decipher the ever-illegible writing of our local Western Union telegraph operator. It read:

Received at: 8:34 P.M

Dated: October 31st

To: Benjamin Whittingham Hathorne

Need expertise. Matters most dire, require your discretion and utmost haste. Meet at sheriff's office in Casper Wyoming at soonest.

(Signed) Arthur C Wilson

"Arthur..."

"Pardon sir?" I had forgotten Tom at my side. I distractedly reached into my jacket pocket and handed him the assorted bills and change found there without counting.

"My thanks Tom, I'll see you inside." He hastened off, to some other chore I expected.

The mental diversion intended by the routine of opening crates filled with new ethnological artifacts to study and catalogue, was suddenly no longer a concern. The telegram had brought back a rush of fond memories.

Arthur and I had attended the same college many years ago and had become fast friends. His unfortunate romance led to our parting ways, and the occasional letter I received touched on little more than the places to which he had traveled and the odd item of geography that he felt might pique my interest. My letters in return, were to him undoubtedly loquacious in the extreme.

Now it seemed my old friend needed my aid. I had only my erudition to offer, and I began to think of the sort of trouble he might have encountered. What I should bring. What I should leave————It would do me well to see him again and shed the overhanging dread of the last few weeks. Yes, I definitely could do with a change of environment.

I hoped that with the long passage of time, I would find my friend restored to his old humour and once again we would have those discussions which had in the past created such febrile debate. In my mind, a timetable formed, two weeks more or less, at least a steamer trunk worth of books covering a diverse array of esoteric topics as were bound to be inaccessible in a backwards frontier town...

A new excitement had formed; travel to a place I had never seen and the possibility of adventure with my erstwhile friend. Yes, the days ahead looked to be wonderful indeed!

Chapter 12
Arthur

Casper, Wyoming - November 1897

Sheriff Henry L. Patton paced his office, his rotund face and pink cheeks belying his age. He had dark hair swept back with a healthy dollop of pomade, handlebar mustache seemingly perched precariously on his top lip. I knew from past experience that his taut jacket hid the arms and chest of a blacksmith. I knew also, after having had the misfortune to see him in his long johns, it was an appearance disproportionate to his thin legs.

Patton turned his ire toward me again. "Something funny Arthur? I'm beginning to think whatever happened in those mountains has left me a witless deputy."

I straightened in my chair, the memory of those few days flooding back in a mixture of fear, sorrow and rage. I was fatigued. Weeks later and I was still trying to make sense of what I had seen, mourn the loss of my colleague and friend, and find a way to marshal help without ending up in a sanitarium. I had seemingly lost what good will I had with the townspeople, and spending an inordinate amount of time in whichever saloon would have me; that final look in Inkton's eyes…

"Deputy!"

"Yes sir. I mean no, there's nothing funny." I had sobered and was now reconsidering my current state of affairs. I wanted to flee. Every time I thought back to that…thing that had made a mockery of Crawley I wanted to flee. I also wanted to blow up the mountainside and eliminate my fears with it.

He stopped his pacing and faced me directly "I've had word from the last rider I sent up to the logging camp. It's abandoned. Now, this convoluted story you've told me about some…thing, Crawley killing our local Indian? It doesn't make sense, and if I hadn't been aware of your whereabouts during these last disappearances, I would suspect you of having gone off the rails and murdered them all."

My face now feeling hot, I quickly stood and faced him. "You're the third sheriff I've served under, and Crawley was the closest friend I had in this piss poor excuse of a town, and you'd suspect me?"

He put his hands up in a placating gesture. "Settle down Arthur, doesn't take much to light your fuse these days. Your behavior has been worrying folks. I know how you and Crawley got on… It's just that there are expectations of this office, and I have nothing to tell anyone."

"I've told you what happened as best as I can describe it. Inkton told me…"

"Inkton was a drunkard and a con man. I can't believe my deputy would believe some yarn he spun about a magical cave that eats Indians."

I could sense my anger beginning to build, as my hands clenched and unclenched tightly. I took a breath, but before I made a career ending move, the sheriff sighed and moved to sit heavily in his chair.

"I'm sorry Arthur. This situation has me wound nearly as tight as you." He looked out his office window into the street. "If what you said is true, what if… What if whatever it is comes here. We have hundreds of citizens spread from the mountain to the Platte and I'm still trying to find likely folks to deputize."

I had resumed smoking after my return to town and needed a cigarette desperately at that moment. I pulled my chair forward and sat.

"I sent a telegram to an old friend of mine from back home. He's a professor of some sort now, but when we were at school together, he studied some outlandish tales and objects. I've asked for his help, and he agreed. I know he's not another gun, but he might be able to help us sort out this thing. He arrives on the evening train."

"You did this without consulting me?" Patton faced me with raised eyebrows. I knew this was now just grandstanding.

"I'll cover whatever costs he might occur, but he was quite keen to come out here and he has a great deal of inherited wealth. The county needn't clutch it's purse for fear of losing a few dollars to save the town."

I'd swear his eyes actually twinkled. "I'm glad to see my deputy returning. Stop by the Grand Central Hotel to talk to the representative from the logging company, I'll be meeting with some prospective candidates today. I'll let you have your expert, but I plan to bring as many guns to bear as I can."

I nodded. Glad to have some purpose, I grabbed my hat and wool coat from the rack and headed out into the street.

Part Two

"Must I then see, alas! eternal night"

Lord Herbert

Chapter 13
Benjamin

Casper, Wyoming - November 1897

I marveled at the skies, violet hues blending into the varied grays of clouds, the fading yellow of sunlight that overhung the hills and mountains to the west. I thought that had my posterior not been flattened entirely during the last stretch of rail from Cheyenne to Casper, the serenity of it would have been breathtaking. As it was, it was merely a mild distraction from the aches of travel. Such vistas I had seen since leaving Salem!

As the train neared the depot, I got my first view of Casper. I wondered at the size of it and began to feel the first stirrings of unease at the thought of so few, struggling to live lives on the plains so far from civilization. I chided myself, surely a hardy and brave people made their living here. And Arthur.

During our early years, the man had had a knack for pulling me away from my books, to carouse amongst the gas-lit streets of the Back Bay. Equally at home among the seedier dives and the College halls. Surely Arthur would have settled somewhere with at least a hint of culture. But years had passed, and the letters I'd received since had done little to reassure me about what changes time had wrought on my crestfallen friend.

The train began its clangorous halt, and I scrutinized the walkway of the depot for my friend. Grabbing my valise, I alighted the car. I made my way through the small crowd toward where the baggage men were unloading, eyes alert for my Saratoga trunk. My attention thus occupied; I was startled when a hand touched my shoulder. I turned, and though the years and recent events had wrought changes, I instantly recognized the man.

"Arthur! So good to see you." I clasped hands and we shook as I took in my friend for the first time in some 15 years.

Arthur was a hands-width taller, perhaps an even 6 foot to my 5'6" frame. His once muscular body seemed to have experienced some recent atrophy and his pallid complexion spoke to some recent affliction. His dark brown hair tousled out from under his hat, a fringe above his still bright hazel eyes. I remembered him always clean-shaven, but he now sported a few days growth.

He had noted me observing his appearance. "I imagine I'm just handsome enough to draw the eye of every third lady at the saloon, which should still put me ahead of you." He smiled and for a moment it was almost as if we were back in Boston, him goading me into some foolish stunt.

"I'm so glad to see you well." I saw him flinch slightly. "Your telegram? It sounded urgent. Have I arrived in time to be of some aid?"

"That remains to be seen." He glanced around the still crowded platform and then grabbed my arm to pull me in the direction of the baggage area. "Let's grab your luggage and we'll go somewhere more private to talk."

Arthur was peering over the heads of the small group of people hustling around the assortment of baggage.

"It's a Saratoga, mahogany trim."

He looked at me with a slight smirk. "Of course it is." He had apparently spotted it, as he began to shoulder his way through. It was then he bumped the arm of a lady pointing out a bag to her companion. He turned immediately to apologize, and I noticed his cheeks suddenly burning crimson.

"My apologies ma'am."

As the lady turned to face Arthur, her profile caught my attention and I realized what had so flustered my friend. As I moved in Arthur's wake, I could then see her full on and she was a beauty in every sense. Ice blue eyes stood out from her alabaster skin; her delicate features framed by light golden curls. A pert upturned nose, above small pink lips. I was suddenly quite mute.

She smiled. "No apologies necessary, sheriff."

So caught up in the emotions of seeing my old friend

I had failed to notice the nickel star pinned to his jacket. I recalled the telegram "Meet at sheriff's office", he had never mentioned his occupation in any of the short letters I received over the years. I couldn't imagine Arthur, here, a frontier deputy sheriff!

A somewhat abashed Arthur, looking at the star as though just noticing it himself for the first time, replied. "I'm actually a deputy sheriff. You'll find sheriff Patton at his office should you need him."

"I hope not to, Mister…?"

"It's Arthur. Arthur Wilson."

I harrumphed. "And this is my friend Benjamin Hathorne."

Spotting my trunk, I bowed slightly and excused myself. Behind me I heard their continuing conversation.

"I'm Catherine, Catherine Metcalf." Her voice was high and musical, but I was determined to be only as polite as etiquette required, as my friend appeared already smitten.

"Pleased to meet you ma'am." He gently took her proffered hand. I wondered at my friend, formerly such a self-assured man, seemingly made timid by this beautiful woman.

She turned to her escort, an older black woman who now carried a piece of luggage in either hand. "Thank you, Eleanor."

"It was nice meeting you both, perhaps we'll meet again in more social circumstances. I believe you know my Father?" This last to Arthur.

"Yes, of course, I've given him my trade from time to time. Enjoy your stay in Casper ladies."

I watched Arthur gape as the two walked towards the front of the depot to alight on their waiting carriage.

"Shall I draw up the wedding announcements?"

Arthur grimaced, glancing back across the track towards the mountains. "It would be better if she boarded the train back to where she came from."

"Now let's get this ridiculous trunk of yours out to the street and see if we can find a coach to carry it."

Chapter 14
Arthur

Casper, Wyoming - November 1897

I helped Benjamin get installed at the Grand Central Hotel. He negotiated for the largest room, probably still considered shabby by his standards, but there was a dearth of options in Casper. I took a seat at the small table and watched as he unloaded books and a motley assemblage of other items onto the bed and dresser. A small case caught my eye.

"Did you come armed?" I was astonished, a more book-ish person I had never met. When at College, I was the brawn, he the brains.

"Yes, I certainly did. Do you recall the particular wording of your telegram?" I shook my head; it had been a few weeks and my mind in a state of panic.

"Dire? Haste? Soonest? My good man, I was certain I would find Casper in ashes when I arrived here."

I lit a cigarette, sudden realization that Benjamin was not only here, but that I had potentially put him in peril. I offered one up to him, but he declined. He pulled up at the other chair and set the case on the table. He grinned impishly.

"Have a look."

I opened the wooden lid and took in what appeared to be a handgun of outlandish proportions. Inside the main compartment, surrounded by smaller partitions that contained tools, powder and other sundries, sat a pistol grip attached to a frame with a parallel set of 5 barrels.

"I got it in London, at a shop on James Street. It's a 10 shot .36 caliber boxed action repeating pistol. What do you think?" His excitement was palpable.

"It certainly is something." I hefted it, turning it in my hand, wondering at the weight of it. "Have you fired it?"

"Of course, it was the talk of the sportsman's club when I brought it in. A wonderful design don't you think?"

I placed it gently back in the case. "If it doesn't blow up in your hand, I suppose it's mighty fine."

He looked briefly downcast, then a knock came at the door, and a barmaid entered at his urging with a bottle and two glasses. He gave her a few coins gratuity and after she had shut the door behind her, he began to pour from the dark green bottle.

"Scotch, I got a taste for it on my travels to Britain. Apparently, the owner had to send out, only one other connoisseur in your little town."

We touched glasses, and I downed mine in a single draught, a feeling of warmth spreading through my body.

"Try tasting it next time."

I poured another. "It is good, better than the swill they usually serve downstairs."

Benjamin set down his drink and folded his hands, looking at me for all the world like a professor gaging a student. Which I suppose was partly true.

"I dropped everything, and now I'm here. What is happening Arthur? What expertise could a deputy sheriff require?"

I took time sipping the second drink, trying to gather my thoughts. Although he hadn't expressly said it, it was obvious he felt slighted by the scarcity of information in our correspondence. About Benjamin I knew a great deal. He had held two professorships, one at Harvard and another, briefly, in Scotland. His interest in the arcane and esoteric had continued, and if anything grown in the intervening years.

"Do you have a sobriquet?"

"Pardon?"

"Arthur 'Slow Toes' Wilson. Or perhaps Arthur 'Shot A Man When He Was Five' Wilson? Something that reads well in the papers."

"Benjamin, I know I have been less than candid in my letters. And for that I apologize. But that needs to be put aside. I wrote for your help, because you were more than candid in yours. I have put all my hope in your vast knowledge of all those things occult and arcane."

Benjamin, leaned forward, suddenly intent. "Tell me everything."

And I did…

Chapter 15
Cody

Deer Creek Range, Wyoming - November 1897

The Allen brothers followed their patriarch through the freshly fallen snow, their horses steaming in the morning chill. The father, Larry, turned back to see that they'd kept pace. Being the youngest, Cody trailed a horse-length behind his brothers, George and Henry, who rode side by side. Both kept their hat brims down and their eyes forward. A bright day like this in the valley, covered in white, and the sun was hurtful to the eyes.

The Allen Ranch lay a couple of miles to the east of the few remaining buildings that once made up the town of Bessemer. The Platte river just a short ride away, when the boys wanted to go fishing. Each of the boys carried Winchester rifles. For the Allen family, a rite of passage into adulthood. Cody had earned his only a month prior. His father carried an old sawed-off 10-gauge double-barrel shotgun that he usually kept around to scare off predators.

They had lost ten head of cattle in the past few weeks, and when his father reported it to sheriff Patton the man actually warned him away from pursuing the cattle thieves into the mountains. According to the sheriff there was a logging camp nearby, and it was the site of some trouble. To Larry Allen, that meant that he had some loggers turn outlaw.

His father had been of a mind that morning to send a telegram to the Marshal's office in Cheyenne, but then Cody had gone out to check on the herd. Seeing three more cattle missing and this time a trail that could be followed, he ran back to the house and breathlessly reported it to his father. The Marshals would take some time to respond, assuming they chose to, and so his father declared that he and the boys would sort it for themselves. Cody looked on as his father kissed their mother and made his promises to be back by dark.

His father was riding some ten yards ahead, in order to see the trail before the passing horses rendered it indecipherable. He was followed a series of indentations, the new snow obfuscating the individual tracks, so that it was hard to make out which was animal or man and how many there were. If it continued on it would enter the tree-line, and he wondered what kind of rustler would try hiding the animals in such a densely forested area. He held up, so the boys could catch up to him.

"Have we run out of trail?" He heard George ask as he brought his piebald mare alongside.

"No son. The trail goes on into those trees. We need to make a decision on how we handle things from here."

Henry lifted his hat slightly to peer into the trees. "I don't see how they could fit our cattle through that brush."

"I had the same thought myself." Larry looked over at his youngest. "Cody, I want you to stay here with the horses. George and Henry will follow me in. If you hear any gunfire, you ride hard back to your Ma, and the both of you ride into Casper to get that lickspittle of a sheriff to finally bring some help."

He wanted to protest, make it clear that he was just as much of a man as his brothers, but like all of Larry Allen's boys, he had been brought up to be mindful of his father. "Yes sir."

He dismounted and gathered their reins and watched as his father and brothers also dismounted and began double checking their weapons. His father glanced over at him and grinned. "Don't worry, these sort are usually cowards, and the sight of three armed men will likely send them running. We'll be back before you can run home to eat all the corn-bread."

His father then turned and began laboriously trudging through the snow and each of his brothers gave him a quick slap on the back before following. Cody watched them, for a few moments their figures were sporadically visible between the trees before disappearing altogether.

Cody sat ahorse to keep his feet warm, as his boots did little in the way of keeping the chill out. He occasionally made a quiet remark to one of the other horses, feeling the need to comfort them. He was looking up at the sky and the landmarks nearby to try to determine how much time had passed, when he heard the distant crack of a gunshot. He stood in his stirrups, gripping his Winchester, his heart pounding in his ears, as he tried to listen for any other sounds.

Suddenly rifle shots cracked out in succession accompanied by the single lower register shout of a shotgun and he watched as birds scattered from the tops of the tree-line. Then the screams began.

Chapter 16
Benjamin

Casper, Wyoming - November 1897

As Arthur finished his tale, the room had begun to darken, his face now barely visible in the gloom. So enrapt was I with the tale that I had hardly noticed the change. I watched Arthur reach for the scotch and as he did so, I moved to get us some light. Finding a bedside lantern, I lifted its globe, striking a match and putting it to the wick. I moved the glowing lantern to a spot just adjacent to the table. I could now make out his features in the pale-yellow light.

"I imagine you probably think I have a slate loose." Arthur's voice hoarse from his nearly non-stop account.

"No. Of course not." I placed my hand on his shoulder and leaned in to make sure my words imparted my true conviction. "I believe it all. I have never known you to lie." I sat back, "I do think you believe yourself a coward for failing to stay and face something that any sane man would flee."

"I was a coward. Poor Inkton fired and continued to fire, while I could barely keep my gun trained on him… It, for all the shaking I did."

"Well if you insist…I shall report your cowardice to Ms. Metcalf forthwith!"

This elicited a small smile. He shrugged. "Nevertheless, that is past and now I hope you have some ideas on what it is we're facing and how to bring it to an end."

Now it was my turn to shrug. "At the moment, I'm not entirely sure. Do you believe the thing had moved from the cave Inkton mentioned by the use of your friend Crawley? Or is there more than one entity?"

"I have no earthly idea, this is your area of expertise, it's why I needed you here. There have been more disappearances since I sent the wire, and Inkton said that back in the fifties the Cheyenne lost quite a few hunters. I don't know if there is an army of things out there wearing our bodies like puppets, or just the one."

I dug through my valise and replied. "I'm afraid my dear Arthur, that what you've stumbled across is something I've only read of in extraordinarily rare books, to which I was privy, only under the watchful eye of certain private collectors." The box I was looking for seemed to have shifted and was proving difficult to fish out. "I have my notes, and I can hope to find something of value there, but my expertise has been, to this point, purely theoretical… Ah!" Having found the box, I placed it on the table between us.

"Some magic talisman?" Arthur looked hopeful and dubious at the same time.

"Of course not, most talismanic magic would require a great deal of ritual for me to create and would likely waste all of our time." Here I paused, remembering the details of his tale. "After all, it sounds like your Indian friend had a medicine bag that proved of little worth against the creature."

"So, what is it?"

I faced the latch towards Arthur and opened the case to reveal its contents to him.

"Ammunition? But what kind?" He was peering more closely, clearly intrigued, here was something that my friend could understand and possibly find comfort in. Within the small box, nestled each in their own cavity, were a variety of .36 caliber ball ammunition. Some with elaborate carvings. Some marbled with different minerals and more esoteric ingredients. Some had undergone the very rituals I had just dismissed for the benefit of my friend.

"An assortment. If my pistol does not 'explode' as you would have it, I have the option of firing 10 different types of shot towards this thing. I can then judge their efficacy."

Arthur sagged back against his chair. "I don't think you understand the unnatural speed at which this thing moved. We probably managed five or six shots altogether and by then Inkton was dead and I was running. I have no doubt that had I stayed; I would not have managed to reload before I ended up dead as well." He granted me a grim smile.

"I can imagine you taking notes between shots as it waits calmly for your analysis."

Undeterred, I continued. "Arthur, we will have to arrange to meet this creature in a venue of our choosing. If we can get enough fire on this thing at a distance, perhaps we can keep it overwhelmed until I can find a suitable way to dispatch it. Perhaps enough gunfire will be all that's needed, and we can go out on the town like old times." Remembering my environs, I looked out of my room window at the few lighted buildings. "Well we can have a drink to celebrate at least."

He was staring at the ceiling, seemingly lost in thought.

"I saw Bella."

For a moment he stayed unmoving and I questioned my reasons for telling him. As a distraction from current events I probably could have chosen something lighter, like perhaps the opening of the Boston subway.

"How is she?" He remained in his position, but I could tell from his stillness that I should have left the subject well alone.

"She seemed well. She inquired after you." I paused, not wanting to cause further distress. "As you know I didn't have much news to tell her, other than you were alive, presumably in good health, and had traveled to the west."

He remained sitting there as though entranced by the pattern on the ceiling. I understood that it was a means of controlling his reaction.

We had been the best of friends when they met. The relationship was tempestuous from the start and ended badly after just a year. He left Massachusetts, and I lost contact with him. Only a letter now and then with few details about himself, just about the places he had been. He knew I had a keen interest in oddities and when he came across them, he would describe the places or events in some detail. I kept them over the years, and had I been inclined could have traced his route across the States.

"Good." He sat forward then and finally met my gaze. "I left all of that behind Benjamin, and I'd thank you not to mention her again."

"Of course, I apologize."

"Now to return to our local monsters, I agree with you on keeping our distance…"

It was just then that a loud knocking erupted at my door. "Deputy Wilson!"

Arthur turned in his seat, reaching the doorknob from his chair, and pulled the door open. The young man there startled mid-knock. "Yes?"

"Sheriff Patton wants to see you in his office right away!"

"What's the urgency?" Arthur had the look of a man condemned.

"One of the Allen boys has come down from the mountains, he claims his whole family has been slaughtered!"

Interlude Three

Deer Creek Range, Wyoming - November 1897

The thing on the slope continued to dream. But the part of it that was consciousness on a level humanity might understand, absorbed and devoured and explored more of this world around it. Its mass now grown overlarge and being averse to direct sunlight, it churned and rolled in a continuous motion like a ball of mating snakes. Its perpetual motion burrowing it further into the mountainside and radically altering the shape of the slope, collapsing its shape into a syncline.

This awareness was now using the flesh of the more sentient beings that it partially consumed; using their understanding, their mobility, their resemblances, to seek out even more sustenance. Using parts of its mass to hollow out the flesh and skulls as it had done to the very rock around it.

Standing about the slope; human figures, who only on closer inspection, might be noticed as different from their kind. For the slick mottled slate mass continued in motion throughout the little remaining flesh and bone and emerged from the orbital fissures to fill the sockets…and see.

Chapter 17

Arthur

Casper, Wyoming - November 1897

I sidled my way past another drunken patron, Benjamin following in my wake, as we made our way out of the saloon that occupied the first floor of the Grand Central. We exited the hotel, turning right down the wooden sidewalk past the jewelry and goods store, dropping off the walk to turn right into the alleyway.

"Try and keep up." I looked back at Benjamin, the flap of his valise open as he tried to organize an array of items to accommodate his strange looking pistol and box of ammunition.

"I hadn't expected to possibly need this so soon." He seemed flustered. His assured demeanor seemingly lost now that we were venturing beyond the theoretical.

"With any luck, we still won't. It's a long ride from here, and it's already dusk. Just let me speak with the sheriff first, he was not entirely pleased when I mentioned I sent for you."

"Sent for me?" Benjamin huffed. "You mean when you

begged me to come to your rescue?"

Even as a young man, Benjamin was the model of Victorian propriety and often came across as supercilious for those who couldn't see through the pretense. For a moment it seemed as if the years were wiped away, if only the wind carried the salt air of the ocean instead of the ripe scents of a frontier town.

"Enough of that. You're not in New England anymore Benjamin and these folks don't know you as I do. Speak plainly, and we should be fine."

"I don't know that I can put De Vermis Mysteriis into simplistic enough terms for your townsfolk. But I shall do my best."

A brief clamor as a long team of mules passed behind us pulling an oil wagon, headed to the depot further down the street. A moment later we exited the alley onto David. I paused for a moment looking south towards Casper Mountain, now barely visible as a series of dark humps one could almost imagine as a monster lying dormant. I motioned Benjamin on to cross the street and vacant lots towards the building where the sheriff's office shared space with the county and city jails.

"Do you know this boy Allen?" Benjamin inquired.

"Not well, they have a ranch some ten or fifteen miles out of town from what I understand. I've seen them in town from time to time, but never had cause to deal with them in a professional capacity." I had sent Patton's errand boy off on another chore before he could gossip around the hotel and didn't bother with further interrogation knowing the sheriff would have told him very little. I had my differences with the sheriff, but he knew what he was about.

"I've noticed that you've adopted the local vernacular." Benjamin now hugged his valise to his chest as we neared the building, his fastidiousness apparent. "I thought for a moment at the depot I was talking to a cowboy out of a dime novel."

"I suppose I've adapted to my surroundings. You wouldn't believe the grief I received when I first arrived here, but I guess I've picked up some of the lingo." I reached the doors and held one open for Benjamin. "If you want to amuse yourself later, get one of the locals to say Worcester."

Once in the entranceway, we could hear the slight sounds of restrained sobbing. I immediately headed to the office on my left, Benjamin following close on my heels. At the door, I again turned to him. "Let me do the talking."

I opened the door without giving him the chance to respond, seated on a bench to the right a lady I assumed to be Mrs. Allen was sobbing into the lapels of the young Allen's jacket. It bothered me that I couldn't recall his name. I looked to the sheriff and he waved us in, Benjamin carefully shutting the door behind us.

"Sheriff, this is Ben…"

"Benjamin Whittingham Hathorne at your service sir." Benjamin placed his valise on the desk Patton was resting against and gave him his hand. They shook, and Benjamin turned and gave me a wink.

"This the ah… Expert you've brought to us from Massachusetts?" Patton fairly chewed on the name of the state.

"Yes sir. I think you'll find he has a grasp on the particular… Problems we're facing." This last said as I looked over at the boy, uncertain of what he had witnessed.

Sheriff Patton looked over his shoulder to where I saw Mrs. Patton sitting at the back desk. She took his non-verbal cue and came forward to take Mrs. Allen's hands. "The missus will see you over to our place. You'll be safe there. The boys and I will look after Cody, we just have a few more questions."

Mrs. Allen looked at Cody, the boy's eyes red from tears, but he looked at her solidly. "I'll be ok Ma."

She nodded, and Mrs. Patton looked back as they passed through the door. Her eyes met mine.

"I expect you to get retribution for what's happened to this boy's family."

I could only look away.

Chapter 18

Benjamin

Casper, Wyoming - November 1897

Unsure of my place but needing to hear all details I moved to sit near the boy. He appeared, perhaps, sixteen. A mop of blonde hair plastered to his face. He seemed a fit boy, if exhausted from the stresses he had encountered. I placed my leather bag close to hand between my feet and set my hand on his shoulder to provide reassurance.

I felt sheriff Patton's gaze on me. "This is Cody Allen. He and his father Larry, as well as his two older brothers George and Henry, headed out after what they believe were cattle rustlers this morning."

"They'd all be alive right now if you'd had come when my Pa first told you about the raids!" I could feel the boy trembling beneath my slight grip. I noticed Arthur looking towards the Sheriff with a look of enquiry. The look on Patton's face made it clear that this was not his first time hearing the accusation.

Deciding that time was of the essence, I proceeded to move events forward. "Hi Cody, I'm Benjamin Hathorne.

I've traveled here from Massachusetts at the behest of my friend Deputy Wilson. I know you're grieving and angry, but you are the best hope we have right now of preventing further deaths."

The boy's hands were clenched tight, his knuckles whitening, but I had his attention now and he slowly began to relax. I glanced at Arthur, and he nodded, content for me to continue with my questioning.

"Now. Deputy Wilson and I have not heard the full account of what transpired today. I know this will be difficult, but it would be of great help to us if you could relate the events again. Leave out no detail, no matter how small. Please." The boy nodded at me, determined to put on a brave face.

Cody Allen began carefully recounting his morning, from his discovery of the missing cattle and the accompanying tracks, to the point of his father and two other siblings disappearing into the tree-line. It was here he paused, having to gather himself, before resuming the tale again. "I heard gunfire, it was hard to tell who had fired, I heard my father's 10-gauge for sure, but I was certain they had found the rustlers and at first I was excited thinking they were finally giving back what we got. But then I heard screams... I had never heard anyone make noises like that before."

"Take your time Cody. The better you recall these details, the more information we'll have."

He took a shuddering breath. "I was scared. I wasn't sure if I should bring the horses closer or run home as father had ordered. I was… Just sitting there, I should have immediately done one or the other, but I couldn't decide to move."

"An understandable reaction, this is not a normal situation. That you're here at all is remarkable." My encouragements seemed to be the impetus he needed, for he continued.

"I finally decided to head towards the trees with the horses in case someone was hurt. I figured Dad would have thought that the right thing to do. The screaming had already stopped. Whatever happened, had happened fast. I was only halfway up the slope when I saw George. He was running towards me; it was heavy snow and I could see that he wasn't able to move very fast. He didn't have his rifle. Somebody was coming up behind him, I just saw a figure, a person, but moving strangely…like their legs wouldn't bend right. George must have heard him, because he turned and reached for his Colt. The man was nearly on him, and he turned and screamed for me to ride and not stop. I started to push the horses, thinking we could both ride away…"

I watched his face wear a mix of emotions, his eyes darting back and forth but not seeing us in the room. It was clear that he was trying to put into words exactly what had happened. "Go on." I gently prodded him.

"George never did draw his pistol all the way. I was

shouting, hoping to draw attention and give him some time. The…man. He changed. It was as though his arms became something else. They shot into George so fast that the very next moment I could see them through his back. Suddenly it was like there were two dark tree roots wriggling there. I drew up hard on the reins. I reached for my Winchester, but then the thing turned its head towards me. Its movements were…not natural. I don't know how to describe it."

Here he stopped to look at me, and I nodded at him to continue, noticing Arthur moving as if in discomfort. "The worst part was the eyes. I know I was probably still a good 50 yards away… But I know. I know it was looking at me. But all I could see was these dark strange…holes where the eyes should be. I gave up then, I left the other horses behind and I rode to the ranch as fast I as could. I got Ma, nearly had to drag her with me. Told her we had to get help. Didn't even hitch the wagon, just had her riding side saddle behind me. Once we neared Casper, a few fellers saw that we were in distress and rode with us, the rest of the way here to the sheriff's office." He angrily wiped at the tears gathered in the corner of his eyes. "That's all I can tell you. Everything."

I was absorbing the information, assembling those parts that matched Arthur and the Indian's tale. Recalling what Arthur had related from Inkton. A picture was starting to form in my mind. I was suddenly feeling very ill-prepared.

"Did you recognize this, this man?" This from Arthur.

"No sir."

"Did you know Deputy Harris?"

I could see Cody, looking as if at something at a distance. "No, I don't think so. We may have seen him when we come into town, but not to speak of."

I looked at Arthur. "So, it likely wasn't Crawley. This means there are more."

Chapter 19

Arthur

Casper, Wyoming - November 1897

I marveled as Benjamin had coaxed the tale out of Cody. Of the two of us, Benjamin had always been the more inhibited. Now it seemed life's experiences had juxtaposed our very temperaments. As events had unfolded here, he'd grown both more self-assured and anxious.

Benjamin stood, glancing down at Cody, and then over at sheriff Patton. "Do you have a place for the boy tonight as well?"

Sheriff Patton, bemused momentarily by this seeming change in authority, rose and knocked at the window. In a moment, Joseph Grange, the same young man who had fetched us from the hotel, entered the office. "Joe, could you escort Cody here over to my place? You'll find his mama already there with the missus."

"Of course, sheriff." Joe held the door for Cody, the latter glancing back as if wanting to say something more, before departing with his head down.

"That poor kid. He's held it together better than I did in the face of these things."

Benjamin sat back down, looking pensive. "Things... I wasn't expecting this."

This was enough for sheriff Patton, he looked from Benjamin to me. "What is going on here? I do believe I'm the sheriff of this county and responsible for the investigation of any parties involved in criminal activities."

Benjamin looked up. "Good luck on making any arrests sheriff. I expect, that we may be seeing you before long as a different being entirely."

"What on earth are you talking about? I don't understand any of this. First Deputy Wilson. Now the Allen kid. Both hysterical and you seem to have arrived there right along with them."

Benjamin looked at him calmly. "I am perhaps uniquely qualified to assist in this endeavour. I won't bore you with my various academic laurels." He had lifted his leather valise and began to rifle through it as he continued.

"I will say that I have traveled and studied widely before my particular...interests brought me back to Massachusetts. There, my position at the Peabody Academy of Science has allowed me to obtain and study things rarely seen and seldom mentioned. Various occult tomes and the apparatus and materials they require."

He displayed the clumsy pistol, five vertical barrels

stacked side-by-side, looking at it admiringly. "Most importantly, I have discovered that there are monstrous things in this world. And by ritual, or by modern invention, I intend to rid humanity of as many as my time on this earth allows."

Patton moved ponderously to take up his seat behind the main desk. I could tell he was out of his depth and continuing on in this fashion would likely just get his back up.

"Henry." The unexpected use of his Christian name drawing his attention. "I've been serving this office from its start. You and I have pulled through enough scraps that I believe I'm entitled to some trust. Benjamin is the only person I know who might have any knowledge of what is up there in those mountains killing our people."

Patton rapped his fountain pen against the desk and looked out through the window, though it only reflected the lamplight and his reflection. A minute or two passed in silence.

"Ok. Ok. What do you suggest we do?"

I left the sheriff's office and wandered down the few streets that made up the town. I had no objective and was just trying to clear my head. Benjamin's plan seemed sound, given the lack of alternatives. Such things shouldn't be. I had been in every den of iniquity from here to the east coast, and never had my courage been found wanting.

I found myself heading back towards Center. I would be staying in town for the evening, assisting in some of the preparations on the morrow, and heading out to my cabin near evening. I stopped for a moment and looked south towards the mountains. It was a cloudless night, and the stars were very bright. One could make out the rare spot of dim light from the lamps that adorned the few inhabited cabins in the foothills. The mountain remained a series of dark humps against the sky.

"Hello Mr. Wilson."

I turned, startled. Ms. Metcalf was standing near to the water pump that abutted the corner of the saloon and alleyway. Her lady was filling a bucket with water.

"Ms. Metcalf," I doffed my hat, recent events having almost driven thoughts of the those sparkling blue eyes out of my mind. "Eleanor."

"Good evening Mr. Wilson." She was puffing a little from working the pump.

"I'd be glad to help with that." Something about Ms. Metcalf made it hard to form coherent sentences and I was looking for a way to delay any conversation.

"No thank you sir, I'm almost finished." She smiled, and I believe she knew just exactly what I was feeling.

I turned back to Ms. Metcalf, and she was also smiling. Thinking of the recent horrors, I was amazed that here stood someone who could so affect me. Laughter spilled out of the building to my right, as a patron stumbled out and began walking southward, before realizing his error and turning back around and left through the alleyway.

"You know the town does get a bit rowdy, especially at night and so close to the saloons."

She giggled, and it aroused an unaccustomed feeling in my chest. "I think we'll be fine. He'd get lost on his way to accost me."

I couldn't help but smile. "Well if you ladies don't mind, I'll stick around until you're finished. There are some men who get a meanness to them after drinking. I know most of them, and they know me."

"Of course…deputy. And please, call me Catherine."

"Yes ma'am, Catherine." I glanced around, unable to maintain contact with those eyes. Every time I looked at her, I wanted to memorize every detail and it was clear that she was aware of my interest and somewhat amused by it.

Something primal in me could not bear the thought of such beauty faced with the horrors of what roamed the mountains. "Will you be staying in town long?"

"Father wanted to have us out for a few weeks, he's anxious to show us how his business is thriving, and to show us what it is that he finds appealing about this part of the country. My mother became ill and had to remain in Dodge City. So, it won't be so very long. My aunt is seeing to her while we are away."

Some years earlier I had spent time in Dodge City, it hardly seemed like the place for a woman like her. These days the paper had few stories of the like I used to read, when men like Bat Masterson roamed the town.

"I don't want to alarm you miss, but we've been having some troubles up in the mountains, and if you're able to return to Dodge City I would do so as soon as you can manage it."

The spot between her eyebrows wrinkled slightly, as she considered this. "My father mentioned some disappearances, but he would insist on me returning if he felt there to be a threat."

"We're privy to some information that hasn't been shared with the town yet, and there is some concern that the troubles may not stay confined there." I wanted her to stay, I needed her to leave. I found her confusing and distracting and wonderful all at the same time.

"Oh." She looked over at Eleanor, who stood next to a full bucket. She had obviously stopped pumping some time before and in my enthralled state I had not noticed. She continued to smile, and I surmised that Catherine often had this effect on men. "Eleanor, lets discuss this with father when we get back."

She turned back to me. "Mr. Wilson, I hope you resolve your troubles and that I have an opportunity to return again."

"I certainly hope so Catherine." Here I paused, and with the kind of courage I sorely lacked on the mountain asked,

"May I call on you if you make it back to town?"

She hooked her arm with Eleanor's and looked at me coquettishly. "Please do inquire with my father while I'm away. If he agrees, I would be glad to." With that, she continued down the street and I watched as they spoke in whispers, an occasional giggle between them.

I realized my heart was beating fast. I continued to watch them, their southward path in the evening light making it seem as though they were disappearing into the darkness of the mountain. I rested the palms of my hands on my Colts.

I now had more than one reason to stop this thing. This time my courage would not fail me.

Interlude Four

Casper Mountain, Wyoming - November 1897

Four figures shambled to a stop on the beginnings of the descent down the north face of the mountain. Under their tattered clothing, strange undulating motions sporadically caused the cloth to stir. Where the remainder of limbs protruded, flesh and bone intertwined with a slick darkened gray substance that now made up muscle and marrow and the very core of what animated these ghastly shapes.

As one their heads bowed towards the nearly imperceptible lights below and far behind them, ever roiling, nestled against the crumbled rock, a vast intelligence stirred within its dreams.

Chapter 20
Arthur

Casper, Wyoming - November 1897

I looked over at Benjamin as we sat in the dark of the coach. He had been trying to write in a small journal using the bit of moonlight that intermittently traversed the interior but was soon jostled into submission. We were headed to my cabin to fetch my rifles and the sheriff insisted on us riding in the hack, with one of his recently deputized men riding shotgun.

Noticing my observance, he turned to me. "I have to capture every detail if possible, it may be of some use to those who come after."

"So. You don't believe we will survive." This tallied with my own thoughts.

"Oh, we certainly have the best of chances. But given what I believe to be our foe… It has had entirely too much time to work undisrupted."

"You fed sheriff Patton a horse load of shit, and we are all going to die. Does that about sum it up?" I expect my grin must have looked cadaverous in the half-light of the carriage.

"No, I believe I have come up with the best possible plan in the circumstances. It is one that, should we fail, will hopefully give us ample opportunity for escape and later use whatever knowledge we have gleaned to make another attempt."

"Now what can you tell me about this 'foe' that you kept from Patton?"

"I did not deliberately keep anything from the man. He just seems to lack the…imagination to fully comprehend what it is that we face."

"So, tell me."

Benjamin again assumed the position I had begun to think as his "professorial" pose. Stock straight against the seat-back of the carriage, his hands folded.

"You were never a particularly religious man as I recall, has that changed?"

"No if anything, the things I've seen have made me less inclined to religiosity."

He nodded, as if confirming already known fact. "Well Arthur, there are in fact 'more things in heaven and earth'. I cannot say for certain based purely on word of mouth, but I believe what we now face is what are referred to in some texts as the Dark Young of Shub-Niggurath. A mouthful I know. This is my hope. Should the thing we face be one of the Outer Gods or another such being, then we are all better off leaving this mountain and perhaps, the entirety of this state to it."

My face must have reflected my obvious incredulity.

"Arthur, this is not exactly a precise science." I could see his frustration at my dubiousness. "Now. I have spent years traveling and compiling notes from texts whose owners were loathe to allow me even a single perusal. These, along with my access to ethnological artifacts and the library inherited from my family, have allowed me to put together what I believe to be a previously hidden system of beliefs that date back to pre-antiquity."

He began to reach into each of jacket pockets in turn.

"Hardly encouraging I know. But. I have notes here from the Liber Ivonis, only recently acquired and not quite fully translated, but helpful still. It describes a sort of entity, a deity of sorts you could say, whose offspring match the description given by you, the Allen boy, and what was recalled to you by your now hopefully deceased Indian friend." He paused here amidst his exited chatter, to try and read from one of the many notebooks he seemed to have secreted about his person.

"Only, there is no mention of them using humankind as an agency for movement. Why would that have changed? Or are we dealing with something else altogether?" He lapsed into distracted silence.

"Benjamin, all of this speculation is meaningless if we cannot destroy it. Did these notes of yours provide the specifics behind your plan?"

"Well yes and no…"

The carriage had stopped sharply. I could hear the agitated whinnies from the pair of horses hitched at the front. I peered out of the opening above the half door of the carriage.

Coming down the road in an unnervingly inhuman gait were at least five persons. It was impossible to see their faces from the inside of the carriage, the lanterns actually occluding my vision. But I was certain they were no longer my neighbors. Drawing both revolvers, I shouted for the driver to turn back.

"We're cut off! Those are the folks the sheriff warned you about!" Given the outlandish nature of the enemy, Patton had chosen to be vague in his direction, and simply implied that Indians or rustlers had been raiding the outlying homesteads.

The driver, seeing the threat, began a wide turn to the right. The wagon road dropping off on the left where it followed along the crest of the hillside. I moved, half leaning over Benjamin, in order to be able to fire. As the wagon noisily lurched into the turn, they gradually came into sight. They were almost loping now, as their human forms were manipulated into impossible motion, the inhabiting organism forcing them faster.

"Fire!" I yelled to the deputy. To his credit, he swung the shotgun at the closest and fired both barrels without hesitation. I began to fire both Colts at the same figure, knowing from experience that we'd be lucky to slow them enough to escape.

I could feel Benjamin trying to reach under me to get to his leather valise and the gun he kept inside. I tried to move. The wagon now righting itself onto the road facing North, the motion of the wagon jostling me about. I grasped at the upholstered back just in time to look out the rear window and see the closest figure lurch and reach out towards us with both arms.

The same writhing pseudo-limbs I had seen pierce Inkton, lashed out towards us, and I quickly jerked my head down, pulling Benjamin with me. I did not breathe for a moment, expecting to feel an unearthly protuberance puncture my flesh. It must have some physical limits, I thought.

The wagon continued its headlong rush down the hillside road, tossing Benjamin and I against the wooden frame and each other, before finally slowing to a more modest pace. I was finally able to regain my seat on the bench and help Benjamin up alongside me. He looked stunned, an object of academic conjecture now frighteningly real.

I felt about my person for any injury and finding none turned my attention to Benjamin.

At that moment, the motion of the coach brought the light of the moon into conjunction, and its beam illuminated the fist-sized hole where Benjamin's head had rested moments before.

Chapter 21

Benjamin

Casper, Wyoming - November 1897

I watched Arthur deftly replace the spent cartridges in each of his revolvers. I rifled through my memory, trying to recall any piece of lore that might better arm us against the incomprehensible things that pursued us.

"Benjamin!" I met Arthur's eyes, just now cognizant that he had been speaking to me for some time. "If you have any ideas, now's the time for them."

I found my mouth dry, incapable for a moment of speaking. "I... I believe that the plan is still our best chance. Only the timetable has changed. We have to hope that the sheriff has been able to marshal the men and supplies."

"If he hasn't, we'll need to light a fire under him. If we even have that much time. We can't rely on these things to be constrained by issues of human stamina."

"No, you're quite right." I relaxed the grip on my pistol slightly, my fingers now numb from the stranglehold I'd had on it since our descent through the foothills.

"Do you know how long it takes for them to… Change people like that?"

"No. What little is written mostly revolves around ceremonies for the worship or appeasement of these beings. There are assorted rituals of protection, all theoretical of course. Various alchemical and metallurgical items to ward off evil. Nothing we have the time for. There are only those items I've brought along."

"Well. We have to hope that is sufficient. The mining camp at Eadsville has been abandoned, but there are other prospecting camps on the mountain, as well as cabins and homesteads… That's a lot of potential bodies."

"These beings… We have to look at them from an entirely singular perspective. Humanity is insignificant to them. They seldom interact in any meaningful way with our world." I sat back, the fear having begun to recede, I started musing. "Now. The Liber Ivonis made mention of a cult and human sacrifice. So far as is known, that cult no longer exists. It's possible that the Cheyenne, and peoples before them stumbled across this being and it took what it was at one time given. It's possible that it is now aware of us in a way that it hasn't been in a millennia. And now grown aware, it's finding use for us as a sort of vessel to inhabit, either to find more nourishment… Or to engulf this world entirely." Having run its course, my ruminations left me more distraught than when I had begun.

"So, what you're saying is that some sort of…'God'? Is going devour us one by one until the entire world has been turned into either one of those things or God-chow? And it's starting with Casper?"

"When you put it that way it does sound somewhat ridiculous."

We had slowed to a stop just outside of town. The coachman stepped down to speak with Arthur. "Where to now?"

Arthur pointed where the road continued into Center street. "Continue into town, we need to find the sheriff." The coachman nodded, hurriedly resuming his position and giving a quick snap of the driving reins to urge the team forward.

"If he followed my suggestion, we should be seeing preparations soon."

Arthur peered out the side, then pointed forward and motioned for me to do the same. I leaned out and looking forward could see hurried activity in the dark. Men and some few women, using a motley collection of freight wagons and cargo to create makeshift bulwarks. "Good, this is good."

"Maybe. We don't know how many there are, and what's driving them may have no use for roads."

I turned to him. "I believe its grasp of this world has been through human intelligence. If so, it will hopefully use that as a basis for its movements. Like us, it may observe an animal's habits in order to hunt it."

"If not, it simply needs to spread out and find us alone."

"Arthur now is not the time for doubts. If we are to save your town, and a certain Ms. Metcalf along with it, I need my cavalier and foolhardy friend of the past."

"You'll have him, for what it's worth."

The coach slowed to a stop, and with the sound of approaching horses, I disembarked to follow Arthur out onto the road. From where we stood, I could see the train depot, also abuzz with industry. Arthur gave the coach a rap and the pair continued on in the four-in-hand.

Arthur held up his hand as sheriff Patton approached on horseback, the few men with him all armed with a variety of shotguns and rifles. Patton wore a look of surprise, clearly not expecting us back so soon. "What's happened?"

"We ran into trouble. It may not be far behind."

"We've barely started to get things in place here." He glanced past us at the people arranging the makeshift fortifications. "I thought we had at least another day."

"I think things need to move much faster apace. If you can hurry folks up, Benjamin and I will fill you in on doings of our 'outlaw' friends."

Sheriff Patton quickly gave orders, and the men with him scattered to deliver his instructions.

"Now, what in the hell happened?"

Chapter 22
Arthur

Casper, Wyoming - November 1897

I began to relate our encounter up in the foothills, when one of the arriving wagons caught my eye. Ms. Metcalf was sitting beside her father on the open back seat.

"What's she doing here?" My heart was suddenly pounding. I had been certain she had taken my warning to heart and was well on her way to Dodge City. A profound fear for her roiled through me. The thought of those remarkable blue eyes turned to a churning blackness.

"Mr. Metcalf offered the loan of his wagon to help move the materials Mr. Hathorne here suggested. His daughter has only arrived in town for a short stay and decided to accompany him. Now can we return to the business at hand, you said there was an urgency to this business."

I drew my attention away, as the wagon continued towards the ineffective looking barrier. "We reached the top of wagon road, maybe a half mile from my place when we ran into them. Maybe five or six, it was hard to tell in the darkness, there could have been dozens more. You might ask your man, he got off both barrels at one of them. Didn't slow it down that I could see. If you need more convincing, take a look at the back of the coach, that hole was nearly Benjamin's head."

Benjamin nodded in agreement, but so far kept silent about the conclusions he had made.

"And how about Mr. Hathorne? Did you fire that fancy pistol of yours?"

"I'm afraid I didn't have the opportunity. Arthur, however, is a very quick shot. He emptied both of his revolvers before I could even draw my weapon. I should say my familiarity with weapons has been entirely confined to sporting clubs." Benjamin said unabashedly. "It will be of more use here, should our plan fall into place."

"We've moved things as fast as is to be expected, given the bunch of lies I've had to concoct to convince folks."

"Get them to move the line about 15 feet and make it fast."

The sheriff looked ready to protest, but then turned and motioned to the deputy who had ridden shotgun on our ill-fated trip up the foothills. He had returned on horseback after leaving the coach somewhere up ahead. He appeared pallid, but still set for duty. Patton had chosen well.

"Ed, what did you see?"

The deputy paled even more. "People. Well they looked like people at first. They walked all wrong. I emptied two barrels of buckshot dead center of one, and he...it kept coming. Then the arms." He paused, clearly uncomfortable relating something he himself had difficulty comprehending. "I'm not quite sure, we were turning in a hurry and it was hard to keep him in sight. But I'd swear I saw them stretch right out to the back of the coach. That's impossible. I know. But that's what it looked like."

For Patton, this was the last bit of intelligence he needed to decide that there was, in fact, an unnatural threat to his town.

"Ed get to the barrier, tell the folks to start digging that line about 15 feet forward, and move fast. If you can lend a hand, all the better. Then take up a position with a good field of fire."

Ed clicked to his horse and moved to deliver the instructions.

He turned toward Benjamin. "Do you have any other ideas?"

Benjamin looked unsure. "As you know, my plan relied on Arthur and the Allen boy only having seen one of these things at a time. I no longer have the luxury of trying to fire multiple shots into a solitary figure to determine the efficacy of the variations of shot that I have loaded." He exhaled, looking defeated. "We now know there are many more moving as a group. I'd say we have to hope they continue on into the town via the road. Whether by dint of the intelligence behind them believing this to be convincing, or due to some residual instinct... That's our best hope. If they split up, we couldn't possibly defend the town. If we had more time, I'd have said we abandon Casper."

"Abandon." Patton spit. "I've sent messengers around town, to advise folks to keep their doors and windows barred and keep any arms handy. I also sent telegrams to the Marshal's office in Cheyenne and to the Governor directly, asking for aid. I implied an impeding Indian attack. It's a shame we no longer have any manned forts in the area. What I wouldn't give to see some cavalry right now."

The sounds of a wagon intruded into our conversation. I was relieved to see Ms. Metcalf and her father heading back into town, their cargo offloaded. "Lock up tight and stay there until you hear otherwise." Mr. Metcalf gave me a quick nod, and Catherine smiled. I felt my face start to burn and could sense Benjamin looking on, obviously observing my reaction.

A sudden commotion at the barricade caught our attention. Someone was riding hard, coming up on us. Patton caught a glimpse of his features. "One of the men I sent out to scout earlier."

He reared to a stop; his horse lathered. "I saw four or five of them approaching. They've made it to the base of the foothills, maybe five or six miles out. I kept my distance as you said, but they're not running. Not moving right either.

Hard to tell from the distance but I'd have said they all had some kind of deformity."

I looked to Patton. "So, we have maybe two hours if they keep to that pace."

"If they stay together, we may just have a chance."

Chapter 23
Benjamin

Casper, Wyoming - November 1897

I walked through my instructions once more. I had noted in my journal the type of shot, and carefully walked through the placement of each ball in the corresponding pistol cylinder a number of times to make sure those firing would hopefully recall the reaction in the heat of the moment. A few of the same make were placed into pockets, my box of unique ammunition now exhausted.

At my request sheriff Patton had sent inquiries for anyone who might have pistols in a .36 caliber. A couple of the residents had Colt Navy's or Percussion revolvers that suited my purpose. More, in fact, than I had ammunition for. I cursed the lack of information but couldn't fault Arthur for not revealing his experiences in a telegram. I had brought the weapon partly out of hubris. I didn't expect to actually encounter a use for it but had made such preparations as an academic exercise and had been hopeful for it to find use in practice. Now I wish I had more time. More information.

I had fully believed that such beings had interacted with us in the past. The artifacts I had collected testified to their existence; utterly unique in their appearance. However, I believed them no longer extant, or supposed them no longer interested in humanity. Such cosmic entities being beyond our human understanding of motive. Having been partly validated in this situation was of no comfort.

"Good luck gentlemen. Please do your best to keep your heads about you. It may be our saving grace." And with that, they headed south toward the now heavily manned palisade.

"One moment Cody." The young man turned back, determination writ on his face. "This may be a losing proposition; you have already done a great deal in protecting your mother. Are you sure you won't reconsider?"

He looked at me, and I could see turmoil of emotions just under the surface. "No sir, this is something I have to do. If you're right I won't be protecting my mother by remaining here. We have to kill these things." Tears were forming at the corners of his eyes, but he refused to show me weakness by wiping them away.

"Fair enough Mr. Allen." He started, and I realized that in spite of events, his position in the remnant of his family hadn't occurred to him. "Best of luck and remember what we've practiced."

He turned to the door, shoulders slumped, following in the footsteps of his cohorts.

Arthur had been seeing to the final details. He and sheriff Patton having concocted a tale of an illness that caused feral behavior. I left them to it. Once battle was joined, they'd know the truth of it. I could only hope the explanation offered them an anchor of sanity amidst the madness.

It was late evening, with very little moonlight to brighten the countryside. They'd placed an assortment of lanterns and torches around the semi-circular fortifications. The lanterns mostly behind the men, and the hastily arranged torches set in irregular fashion along the roadside to illumine our foe. As per our request, roughly some fifteen feet in front, a small blackened channel at times reflected the torchlight. Men stood to the side, torches lit.

There was a shout, and I hurried from the train depot which served as a makeshift headquarters. If we were to suffer a defeat it was to be our rally point. I could see the men clearly in the lantern light, rifles were being put to shoulder and I began to run the short remaining distance to stand beside Arthur towards the middle of our bulwark.

"What news?" I asked, puffing from the short jog.

He continued to look forward, holding a Sharps rifle at port arms. "A scout returned a moment ago, he said they were right behind him. We have moments."

I could see the tension in my friend. They could simply choose to move around us or spread out and we'd be lost before the night was out. I hoped my guess was correct, or that they'd simply see a large group of people as an opportune target of its predations.

A murmur reached us, as men first saw shapes at the end of the torchlight.

"There." Arthur pointed. From my position I could just make out their legs, then as they continued forward into the boundary of circular light, their torsos and finally... Their faces.

There were scattered gasps as their faces were revealed. The flickering light casting their features in an infernal interplay of shadow and revelation. The flesh distorted, eyes blackened orbs, and jaws held in a bizarre rictus, as the thing within had assembled them into a mockery of human form.

They moved up as one, their motions so utterly wrong. Each head moving in unison to slowly gaze at the palisade, the makeshift fortifications, and men manning them. I wondered what the intelligence behind them perceived at that moment. Did the alien thing recognize human defenses? Had it retained the knowledge of the people whom it now used to go about its vile purpose?

My speculation was cut short as they resumed their forward motion. Arthur shouted. "Now!"

The men moved quickly; torches cast to light the oil which filled the hastily dug trench. The figures continued undeterred through the flames. Their horrific appearance now made even more terrible as flesh began to char, some of it still aflame as they passed through the inferno. The gyrations of the underlying darkened mass now causing the forms to become even more misshapen. Unable to retain their mimicry and creating an even more horrific tableau.

Gunfire erupted around me, startling me from my frozen horror. If a command to fire had been issued, I had not heard it. So enrapt had I been at their appearance.

Their forms were held still for a moment, the combined firepower of large caliber weaponry able to push them back irregardless of their seeming inability to cause them injury. This was all part of the plan Arthur and I had hurriedly assembled. I had to now do my part. I stood against a wagon frame and using it to steady my aim began to methodically fire my pistol, counting in my head as each round exited into my target. I had only fired the third shot when all dissolved into chaos.

Black tendrils shot out, no longer able or content to use the guise of human appendage. They were still at a distance and thankfully unable to pierce human flesh. Gunfire continued but it was no longer as focused. Each man reloading as quickly as their fear or bravery allowed them. Shouts adding to the cacophony, I sensed motion behind me, as a few men broke ranks and ran. I could only hope that those firing the specially equipped pistols retained their positions.

Whether by conscious decision or an animalistic need for survival, they charged in different directions. Half human, half monstrosity, they seemed to pick out individuals as targets and rushed towards them, an incongruous mix of fluid and awkward motion that was hard to reconcile. Amidst the lantern light and gunfire, it was hard to focus on them. And now screams began to add to the din.

I had little time to see what was befalling our comrades, as one was heading directly toward Arthur. He was placing his cartridge but would clearly not be able to fire. He came to the same realization and as a long limb shot forward, he raised the rifle to deflect it. It hit the stock and it burst into splintered pieces, its blow slowed but not stopped it hit Arthur, sending him wheeling behind the barrier. All this in a moment, but it had brought the unearthly thing within reach of my pistol and I fired as fast as it's mechanism would allow.

In a sudden burst of eldritch light, the thing came apart. It made not a sound, but simply came apart in fragments. The darkened parts of it's being dissolving to earth, leaving nothing but small fragments of human bone and flesh.

I exulted, and then realized in my panic I had lost count of which barrel had fired. I was trying to quickly observe the position of the hammers, as in the chaos men were screaming and dying around me.

"Five!" came the sudden shout. Cody, he was well and had kept his calm and his count!

I silently thanked God. "Five!" I yelled in response. I heard at least one other shout and knew we might have the smallest of hopes.

I quickly reached into the pocket that held the one remaining ball of that type. It was a small ball of silver, carved with sigils during the alignment of the heavens as was defined by Abdul Alhazred in that rarest of texts. This had been further encased with lead to make suitable munitions. This I loaded into an emptied barrel, long practice making quick work of it. Placing a cap on the nipple and setting the hammer, I looked about to see where I could be of aid.

Not seeing any of the creatures to my right, I turned to the left. A man was screaming, his torso punctured, the foul thing churning through his bowels to inhabit him. It was a nightmarish scene, the fire and lantern light making me feel as though I suddenly inhabited the darkest corners of Bosch's most infernal work. I quickly closed and fired a round into it. It was a repetition of the last entity's demise, only this time leaving a man eviscerated. He fell limp to the ground.

Out of effective ammunition, I looked fearfully about for more of the creatures. The firing had mostly ceased some time before, as men were afraid of hitting their fellows. I could not see anyone engaged with the monstrous things. I tried to locate the source of the remaining fire. Two or three men had moved to the front of the palisade and were firing south, as the last thing moved like a shadow across the road and into the darkness.

It was only then that I recalled. "Arthur!"

Chapter 24
Arthur

Casper, Wyoming - November 1897

The morning light flickered in, its warmth bringing me to awareness. Images of horror flooded my consciousness, and I tried to rise, pain shooting through my upper right side. My right arm was immobile.

"Arthur, it's alright." I looked up to see a weary and grimy Benjamin sitting in a chair beside the bed I found myself in. "We're back in the hotel. I'm afraid there were more injured, and I offered the use of my room."

"What happened?" My throat grated, it was dry and painful. Benjamin handed me a glass of water.

"Your quick reaction prevented the creature from skewering you and making you into a more verbose and cheerful version of my friend." Benjamin's wit was clearly undimmed by the evening's horrors. "We lost three men, more than twice that wounded. The mental toll may be worse, though the sheriff and I tried our best to placate people with a more natural explanation."

"Patton survived?" I couldn't imagine the man dying,

and I expected him to continue to be the primary cause of my misery for some time to come.

"Indeed." Here he paused, clearly for affect. "Although… There was a woman who came to tend you. A Ms. Metcalf I believe. Your injuries should heal well. The shoulder was dislocated, and you have a few broken ribs. Possibly a slight concussion from your knock on the ground. Try not to undo her work."

I felt elated and also horrified. I must have looked a real mess. I gave a snort, a man of my age and temperament having worries over a woman.

"Ms. Metcalf…" I trailed off as the images of the night returned. "How were they stopped?"

At this Benjamin lost a little of his air of nonchalance. "It was the round we designated as number five. A combination of silver and arcane ritual. I couldn't say whether both were required, and it will be some time before I can replicate its creation. Every last round was spent either in the destruction of the attacking monstrosities or fired somewhere into the countryside. Which is rather unfortunate."

I looked at him questioningly.

"One of them got away."

Chapter 25
Benjamin

Deer Creek Range, Wyoming - December 1897

The men began unloading the wagon at the end of the lumber trail. A light snowfall was beginning to cover the ground and collect amongst the trees.

I dismounted and scanned the mountainside. I realized that I would have to walk beneath the trees, which filled me with no small amount of dread. But I needed to see this through. Perhaps my sleep would at last be undisturbed by nightmares.

A man approached in uniform. From the Army Corps of Engineers then.

"Mr. Hathorne?" I nodded. "We're ready when you are."

I gestured for him to lead the way. We began a circuitous path that hugged the mountain slope, encased on either side by trees, or at least so it felt.

I should have felt somewhat secure. This area had been carefully scouted in groups, instructed in the necessary precautions. These were usually led by sheriff Patton or Arthur, who insisted on it although his injuries were still healing. I believed he also needed this resolution. At this moment I hoped he was in the company of Ms. Metcalf. Her attentions to his well-being had led to them finding other reasons to associate with each other. It was time for him to find some happiness.

We turned at last around a slight bend and slowed to a stop. The engineer handed me a pair of leather wrapped binoculars. He then pointed out the direction of our objective. Using the glasses, I could see a slope, the rock looking partly collapsed around a central blackened depression.

The sheriff had called in debts, and we had spent a great deal of time on convincing both the townspeople and outside help of the verity of an highly contagious organism causing diseased and insane behaviours. Originating from a cave on the slope of this very mountain. I had silently thanked the recent bouts of phthisiophobia and a general willingness of people to accept a story, no matter how outlandish, in favor of the very tangible reality of cosmic entities observing and sometimes interacting with our world.

"Do it." I said handing the glasses back.

A series of whistles passed across the mountainside. Then began a rumbling as the mountainside fell, trapping whatever lie in it. Hopefully never to awaken again.

Epilogue

Deer Creek Range, Wyoming - December 1897

The mass roiled as the part of it that had returned from outside was absorbed into its greater being. It assimilated those lesser thoughts, and they too became part of the dream. The part of it that persisted in the outside was only a fraction of its greater whole.

When the mountain came crashing down to enclose it in total darkness. that part felt an almost human anger and for a moment... Nearly awakened from its dreams.

Acknowledgements

The germ of this novella was a discussion over the lack, or at least my perception thereof, horror westerns. Robert E. Howard wrote the wonderful Horror From the Mound and I had encountered a few others of varying quality over the years. My grouching resulted in my girlfriend suggesting that I write a book on the subject myself. And so, I fired up my computer and began to write.

As Howard himself had sometimes done, I borrowed some of the mythos from his friend H.P. Lovecraft. The rest was a mixture of historical research and my time spent in most of the various locations. My father's encyclopedic knowledge of historical firearms was invaluable. If there are inaccuracies, they are all my own.

About the Author

Max Beaven is an accomplished misanthrope. This is his first book.

Other books by this author

Please visit your favorite ebook retailer to discover other books by Max Beaven:

The Arthur C. Wilson & Benjamin Hathorne Series
Dark Lantern of the Spirit
Grim Oceans, Savage Plains (coming soon!)

Standalone
The Internet of Wicked Things (coming late 2021)

Connect with the author

Thanks for taking the time to read my book, if you found it enjoyable and would like to learn more please visit my website: maxbeaven.com

9 781736 636213